DISCARDED BY NEWSTEAD PUBLIC LIBRARY

Fade to black . . .

"Places, everyone . . . and . . . action!"

Frankie had scarcely made her entrance when a voice bellowed, "Cut!"

Everyone turned to the director, but he still sat in his folding canvas chair, his megaphone on the floor beside him.

"Whash—wha's going on here?"

Arthur Cohen staggered forward, his tie crooked, his face flushed. The soundstage was warm from the spotlights, but surely not so hot as to warrant the beads of perspiration that dotted the producer's forehead.

"Martinis for lunch, eh, Artie? Wish I'd been invited," the director, Mr. Harrison, quipped in a jovial voice that didn't quite ring true. "Tell you what, why don't you go back to your office for a bit of a nap, and this evening we'll take a look at the rushes. I think you're going to be pleased."

But it was clear that Arthur Cohen was *not* pleased. His rant grew louder and more incoherent.

"You remember who signs your check!" Cohen wagged a pudgy finger in the actor's face. "*I'm* the one in charge here, not you, and not Maury, and not my wife! *I'm* the one who—I'm the one—I'm—"

His face turned an ugly shade of purple, and then Arthur Cohen fell forward, landing with a thud at Frankie's feet.

DISCARDED BY HEMPSTEAD PUBLIC LIBRARY

Also by Sheri Cobb South:

IN MILADY'S CHAMBER
A DEAD BORE
OF PAUPERS AND PEERS
THE WEAVER TAKES A WIFE
BRIGHTON HONEYMOON
FRENCH LEAVE
MISS DARBY'S DUENNA
THE COBRA AND THE LILY
THE CHANCE OF A LIFETIME

BABES IN TINSELTOWN

A MYSTERY OF HOLLYWOOD'S GOLDEN AGE

BABES IN TINSELTOWN
Copyright 2012 by Sheri Cobb South. All rights reserved. No
part of this book may be used or reproduced in any manner
whatsoever without written permission from the author, except
in the case of brief quotations embodied in critical articles or
reviews.

Cover illustration ©Gorbash Varvara/Shutterstock.

BABES IN TINSELTOWN

A MYSTERY OF HOLLYWOOD'S GOLDEN AGE

SHERI COBB SOUTH

Mystery
Fic
Cobb

3 1764 00422 0772

Acknowledgements

Stepping outside one's comfort zone is never easy, and can sometimes be terrifying. In my case, after having written seven novels set in early nineteenth-century England, I felt compelled to try my hand at a mystery set in Hollywood in 1936—a project all the more intimidating when I considered that there are people alive today who would know if I got something wrong. Clearly, research was of the essence. I would be remiss if I neglected to mention the contributions of Dr. Georganne Scheiner, Chair of the Women and Gender Studies Program at Arizona State University, who generously sent me photocopies of her research into the Hollywood Studio Club; Elizabeth White, critique partner extraordinaire and all around good friend; my daughter Jessamy South, who volunteered her services as beta reader; and my parents, Bill and Jayne Cobb, who were asked to dredge up their earliest memories of growing up in the South in the late 1930s and '40s. If, in spite of all their best efforts to keep me straight, I still managed to get things wrong, feel free to place the blame squarely on my shoulders.

BABES IN TINSELTOWN

1

Strangers on a Train (1951)
Directed by Alfred Hitchcock
Starring Robert Walker, Farley Granger,
and Ruth Roman

Aboard the Pioneer Zephyr, *1936*

Told you so . . . told you so . . . told you so . . .

To nineteen-year-old Frankie Foster, hurtling through Oklahoma at a blistering speed of forty miles per hour, the rhythm of big wheels on iron rails was strangely reminiscent of her mother's voice. Not that Mama would be so cruel as to say "I told you so." No, instead she would give her youngest daughter the pitying glances and sad, sympathetic smiles that were worse than any amount of scolding.

But then, her mother had never really understood Frankie's fascination with the movies. To Mama, Hollywood was only one step removed from Sodom and Gomorrah. "All that smoking and drinking," she'd fretted when told of her daughter's ambitions, "to say nothing of the s-e-x." This last was said with a furtive glance at her husband, as if the Honorable Hubert Foster might hand down Solomonic wisdom from the judge's bench, yet be wholly ignorant of how his three daughters had been conceived.

In the end, it had been Esther, the colored woman who had cooked and cleaned for the Fosters as long as Frankie could remember, who had come to Frankie's rescue.

"Children gonna grow up, Miz Foster, and there ain't nothin' you can do about it," she'd said, dispensing homegrown wisdom along with mashed potatoes and gravy. "Can't hold back the tide, so you might as well go with the flow."

And that, eventually, had been that. But now the green Georgia hills had given way to flat brown plains, and the trip that had once seemed so exciting now appeared a frightening leap into the unknown. She found some small comfort in the fact that she was not the only one making such a journey. During the occasional stretches where the tracks ran alongside Route 66, she could see sad-looking processions of heavily laden Model T's bearing grim-faced men and weary women. These were the people described by the newsreels as Okies, those displaced farmers who had abandoned their draught-ridden lands in search of greener pastures in California. Would they understand her need to go there, she wondered, or would they say she was crazy to leave a comfortable home with a loving family?

With a screech of the brakes, the train lurched to a stop.

"Tulsa!" bellowed the conductor. "All out for Tulsa!"

Half a dozen passengers disembarked and twice as many new ones pushed their way aboard, scrambling for the few remaining seats. Not for the first time, Frankie was thankful her mother had insisted on a private compartment. Once the new passengers were safely on board, the train jerked into motion again. Frankie settled back in her seat and cracked open her brand-new copy of *Gone with the Wind*, the book everyone seemed to be talking about. She had paid a whole three dollars for it at the St. Louis station, but the purchase had made a statement of sorts: Mama had never let her read it back home, claiming it was full of filthy language. Frankie wasn't quite sure how Mama knew this when she hadn't read it herself, but her mother seemed to operate on the principle that anything that popular must be immoral.

She had hardly read more than a paragraph or two when the sliding door to her compartment slammed open and a broad-shouldered young man in a letterman's sweater burst in.

Frankie looked up from her book. "I'm sorry, but this is a

private—"

"You've got to help me," he interrupted breathlessly. "They'll be coming after me, see?"

"Why?" Wide-eyed with apprehension, Frankie suddenly remembered everything Mama had ever told her about the dangers that might befall a young woman traveling alone. Still, this young man didn't look like a criminal or an escaped convict or a madman. True, his soft felt cap and the V-necked sweater worn over his shirt and necktie were more casual than the flannel suit and fedora favored by most rail travelers, but after two days spent in stockings and heels (to say nothing of foundation garments), Frankie felt this circumstance was more to be envied than condemned. "What have you done?"

"I jumped the train," he said, as if that should explain it all.

"You're not supposed to jump on trains?" asked Frankie, bewildered by the unexpected intricacies of railroad etiquette.

He grinned, revealing two deep dimples. "Sure you can, as long as you've got a ticket—which I don't."

"Oh!"

As if on cue, the conductor's voice floated down the passage calling, "Tickets, please! Tickets!"

"Uh-oh, looks like you're done for," said Frankie, not without sympathy.

The stowaway gave her a measuring look, then stole a

furtive glance back down the passage. "Maybe. Then again, maybe not."

Ignoring her sputtering protests, he pulled the door shut behind him and flung himself down on the seat beside her, knocking them both backward until she was lying prone on the seat with him stretched out on top of her.

"Sorry, toots, but this is a matter of life and death."

With that, he pressed his mouth to hers just as the conductor rapped on the compartment door.

"Tickets, please!"

The conductor, hearing no response from within, rapped again. Still no answer.

"Tickets, please," he said again, sliding the door open. "Tick—"

He froze. Inside the compartment, a young couple lay locked in a passionate and, yes, *horizontal* embrace, the young woman all but invisible except for a pair of slender stocking-clad legs writhing and kicking in such a way that the skirt of her blue suit was rucked up to her knees.

"Sheesh!" muttered the conductor, backing into the corridor and closing the door. "Newlyweds! You'd think they could at least wait until dark!"

Her attacker did not release her right away, but waited until the conductor's call for tickets faded down the corridor before sitting up. "Whew! That should do the trick."

"How dare you?" Frankie sputtered, painfully aware of the fact that she sounded like the heroine of a Victorian melodrama instead of a modern twentieth-century woman. To cover her own embarrassment, she made a great show of straightening her skirt, tugging at the peplum of her belted jacket, and adjusting the angle of the tiny blue hat perched atop her fashionably marcelled brown hair.

"I said I was sorry," he reminded her.

"You also said it was a matter of life and death. I didn't believe you then, either." As if to prove the point, she scrubbed at her abused mouth with the back of her gloved hand. Mama said a lady should always wear gloves, but Frankie hoped she never had to explain how this particular pair had become stained with lipstick.

"It's true," he insisted. "I've got to get to Nevada, but my Tin Lizzie died along the way, and I don't have time or money to waste in fixing her. So I hopped the train."

"Are you one of those Okies?" asked Frankie, curious in spite of herself.

He bristled at the perceived insult. "Not on your life! I just graduated from Texas A & M with a degree in engineering. I've got a job at the Boulder Dam waiting for me. A good engineer can earn over two thousand dollars a year, you know. By the way," he added, holding out his hand, "the name's Mitch Gannon. And you?"

Frankie hesitated for a moment, then offered her gloved fingers with the air of one bestowing an undeserved favor. "Frances. Frances Foster. I'm an actress."

His eyes widened in admiration. "No kidding? What pictures have you been in?"

"None yet," she admitted, wishing she didn't sound so apologetic. "I'm on my way to Hollywood."

"I see."

Something in his tone suggested he saw a great deal more than she had intended. She tossed her head, and immediately regretted it as her little blue hat lurched sideways. "Just because I've never made a picture doesn't mean I'm completely lacking in experience. Why, I'm known all over Georgia as the Snowy Soap Flake girl." It wasn't a lie, exactly. Anyone with a radio tuned to an Atlanta station would know the jingle, even if they'd never thought twice about the girl who sang it.

"The what?"

"The Snowy Soap Flake girl," she repeated impatiently. "You know, like on the radio: 'For whiter blouses, shirts, and socks, Gentle enough for your frilliest frocks, Only fifteen cents a box, Try new Snowy Soap Flakes.' "

He shook his head. "Never heard of 'em. But if they ever

17

make a movie about laundry detergent, I'll bet you'll be a shoo-in for the starring role." With this assurance, he rose from the seat and reached for the door.

Frankie was suddenly and perversely reluctant to see him go. Rude and arrogant he might be, but his was the first friendly face she had encountered since leaving Atlanta. Her cheeks grew warm at the memory of just how friendly he could be. Still, surely even his company was better than being alone.

"Where are you going?"

He jerked a thumb in the general direction of the dining car. "Out to see if I can snag a pack of cigarettes."

Frankie's eyes narrowed in suspicion. "I thought you didn't have any money."

"I didn't have enough money for a ticket. But I won a little bit back at Tulsa station, pitching pennies with the porters. I should be able to come up with fifteen cents for a pack of Lucky Strikes, anyway. Thanks again for all your help."

With one last grin and a wink, he was out the door. Frankie watched it slide closed behind him, her bosom swelling with indignation. *Thank you for all your help.* As if she'd had any choice in the matter! He was just the sort Mama had always warned her about. Besides being rude and arrogant, he gambled and smoked cigarettes. She thought of that other vice, the one Mama could not even bring herself to speak aloud. Was it possible that he—? Then she remembered the way he had kissed her, and decided that *nothing* he might do would surprise her.

Many miles later, the train drew into the Pasadena station with a long hiss like a sigh of relief. Frankie stuffed Scarlett and Rhett back into her purse, then stood up and stretched her cramped muscles. She picked up the jacket she'd shed somewhere around Albuquerque, shrugged her arms into the sleeves, and gathered her bags. As she exited the train, a red-capped porter offered to take them, but she shook her head. Mama, she knew, would disapprove of a lady hauling her own luggage, but in spite of what Frankie had told the presumptuous Mr. Gannon, she was not at all certain she would find work quickly. Better to save what money she had, and let the porter earn his tips elsewhere.

Outside the station, she blinked. Spring had scarcely touched the mountains of northern Georgia, but here the sun shone blindingly bright on green palm trees and scarlet hibiscus swaying in the gentle breeze beneath a brilliant blue sky. The colors were almost too beautiful to be real, like the picture postcards friends sometimes sent from Rock City or Florida or even Niagara Falls, and which always made her feel envious because her friends were traveling and seeing the world, while she was sitting at home reading postcards.

But this was no postcard, and it was no vacation. However strange it might be, this was home now. Somehow she had expected it to feel more familiar, more welcoming. She remembered seeing the old newsreels of Greta Garbo arriving at this very same station. There had been a man to meet her—Frankie couldn't remember who he was, but she was sure he'd been somebody awfully important—and he had given her an enormous bouquet of roses, and they'd both smiled for the cameras. Frankie didn't expect to be met with an army of photographers, much less an armful of roses. Still, she'd never imagined her glamorous new career would begin this way, with her standing beside the curb alone and lost, like a discarded mattress or an old Frigidaire.

"Pardon me, little lady, are you looking for someone?"

Frankie turned and saw a short, stout man bearing down on her. He was wearing a pin-striped suit with a gold chain swinging from his watch pocket. A cigar dangled from one corner of his mouth.

"I—I've just arrived," Frankie explained quite unnecessarily, given the pile of luggage at her feet. "I'm still trying to take it all in."

"You're an actress, right?" The stogie bobbed up and down as he spoke.

"Yes, I am," said Frankie, pleased and gratified to be

recognized as such. "How did you know?"

"You've got the look, kid. You'll go far. Yes sir, you stick with old Herbert Finch, and he'll make you a star." He thumped his chest, giving Frankie to understand that he himself was "old Herbert Finch."

"Can you do that?" asked Frankie, regarding her new acquaintance with wide-eyed admiration.

He removed the cigar with pudgy fingers, then laughed, revealing a gold-capped tooth. "Can I? Honey, I've been making stars for more than a decade. Louis B. Mayer, Irving Thalberg—all of 'em come to old Herbert when they need fresh talent. Hey, but I mustn't keep you standing here. You must be starved after your trip."

"No, no," Frankie hastened to reassure him. "I'm in no hurry, Mr. Finch—no hurry at all!"

"Call me Herbert. Say, let's go get a bite to eat, and we'll talk about your future in the movies." He gestured toward a sleek black Studebaker parked beside the curb.

Mitch Gannon, observing this scene from a distance, hefted a dented footlocker onto his shoulder and tapped the shoulder of a freckle-faced porter very nearly his own age.

"Hey, who's the suit?"

The porter followed the direction of his gaze until he

spotted Frankie and Finch. "Fellow talking to the doll in blue? Calls himself Herbert Finch. He hangs out at the station looking for slick chicks traveling solo." He lowered his voice to a conspiratorial whisper. "From what I hear tell, he promises to make 'em famous, then once he gets 'em alone—*fffft!*"

Mitch didn't have to ask for a definition. "Not this one, he's not!" He ground out the words through clenched teeth. "Flag me a taxi, will you? I'll be right back."

Without hesitation, he strode across the platform and seized Frankie by her blue-clad elbow.

"C'mon, honey, I've got a cab waiting."

"But—but—" Her gaze fell on the trunk balanced on his shoulder. "Where'd *that* come from?"

"Don't change the subject." Ignoring her outraged protests, he picked up the largest of her bulging suitcases and set out for the nearest taxi stand.

Frankie cast an apologetic glance at the sputtering Herbert Finch. "Oh dear! I'm sorry—I'd better—where can I reach you?"

Finch made no reply, but muttered something under his breath and took off in the direction of a shapely young blonde farther down the platform.

"I hope you're happy now," Frankie scolded Mitch as she joined him at the waiting taxi. "I was just about to have lunch with a real live talent scout!"

"Tell it to Sweeney," recommended Mitch, unrepentant. "Didn't your mother ever tell you not to talk to strangers?"

"You mean like the kind you meet on trains?"

The porter cleared his throat. "Maybe it's not my place to say, miss, but if you ask me, it's a good thing your boyfriend came along when he did. That Mr. Finch, he's a bad egg if there ever was one."

"He's not my—what do you mean, a bad egg?"

"He's always hanging around the station watching the trains come in. When he sees a pretty girl traveling alone, he offers to make her a star."

"What's wrong with that?" Frankie asked. "Everyone could use a little help in starting off on a new career—except, of course, people who throw away perfectly good jobs to go following other people where they're not needed or wanted," she added with a darkling glance at Mitch.

Mitch acknowledged this verbal thrust with a grin, but the porter's expression grew even more solemn. "Oh, he gets them started on a new career, all right, but not the one they came to California for."

Frankie, bewildered, would have asked for an explanation, but Mitch threw open the back door of the taxi with a flourish.

"Madam, your chariot awaits."

The taxi driver, waiting at the wheel with an expression of patent boredom on his weathered face, tapped the ash from his cigarette to the pavement below. "Where to, miss?"

Frankie hesitated, not knowing how to answer. Mitch regarded her with raised eyebrows and an infuriatingly smug smile. Once again it was the porter, stowing her suitcase into the taxi's trunk, who came to her rescue.

"If I were you, miss, I'd try the Hollywood Studio Club on the corner of Lodi Place and Lexington. The rent's cheap, and it includes two meals a day." Sensing that these attractions were insufficient to tempt her, he added, "Myrna Loy used to live there, you know." He slammed the trunk closed as if to emphasize the point.

"Oh, I loved her with William Powell in *The Thin Man!*" Frankie enthused. "All right, the Hollywood Studio Club it is. And thank you so much—you've been so very helpful!"

She pressed a dime into his palm, and bestowed upon him a smile so dazzling in its brilliance that the hapless porter was reduced to blushing incoherence. With a jaunty wave of one gloved hand, she swung herself into the back seat of the taxi and began straightening her skirt.

"Turn down the wattage before you electrocute the poor guy," recommended Mitch, giving her a nudge.

"What are you doing?"

"I'm sharing a taxi with you, remember?"

Frankie slid over grudgingly. "I thought you were getting off in Las Vegas."

He shrugged. "I changed my mind."

"But you had a job waiting!"

"Yeah, well, maybe I have a hankering to work in the movies."

Frankie gave a disdainful sniff, and fixed her attention on the passing scenery. Mama, she knew, would be appalled at her lack of manners, and with good reason: Frankie shuddered to think what might have happened to her if she'd gotten into Herbert Finch's car. Now, alone with her rescuer, she found herself strangely at a loss for words. She was more than a little embarrassed at having so easily fallen for what should have been an obvious trap, and chagrined to think that the first person she should meet on her big adventure probably thought she had no more sense than a—than a—

"Oh, look!" Frankie's self-consciousness was instantly banished by the sight of huge white letters spelling out HOLLYWOODLAND against the distant green hillside. "I'm really here! Somehow it didn't seem real until now."

Her enthusiasm was contagious, and Mitch entered into it wholeheartedly. She had apparently decided to forgive his officious behavior at the station, and as long as she was pelting the taxi driver with questions, she was unlikely to press him on certain subjects he would prefer to avoid. After all, what possible explanation could he give for chucking a perfectly good job and lighting out for California, all because of a girl he happened to meet on a train? Okay, so maybe he'd done more than meet her. Still, she wasn't the first girl he'd ever met—ever kissed, either, for that matter. That was no reason for him to become her self-appointed protector. Besides, any amorous pursuit of Frankie Foster was doomed from the start. If ever a girl was the Marrying Kind, it was Miss Pure-as-the-driven-Snowy-Soap-Flake Frances Foster, and he'd never met a girl less interested in marriage—except for maybe Barbara Malone, the toast of the A&M locker room, but Babs was a different class of female altogether.

So there was no logical explanation for his actions except that he was a complete lunatic—and yet, if he had it all to do over again, he would do the same thing. *Somebody* had to look after the girl and make sure she didn't jump into the car with every Tom, Dick, and Harry who offered to make her a star. It might as well be him. And if her dreams of Hollywood stardom came crashing down around her, somebody would have to pick her up, dust her off, and put her back on a train to Georgia. He could do that, too; he'd always heard it was pretty country.

2

Girl Crazy (1943)
Directed by Norman Taurog
Starring Judy Garland and Mickey Rooney

The Hollywood Studio Club proved to be a three-story building in the Mediterranean style, with a red tile roof and a painted frieze over the three arches that framed the front door. As she entered the foyer with Mitch at her heels, she was struck by the soaring ceiling with its exposed beams, the airy rattan furnishings interspersed with potted palms—and the sheer number of females. They were everywhere: draped over the rattan chairs, clustered around a prominently displayed bulletin board, flitting up and down the stairs. From somewhere in the distance came the tinny sounds of a radio playing "Anything Goes," while the rhythmic thumping of footsteps overhead indicated that the next Ginger Rogers or Eleanor Powell hopeful was hard at work.

"Good afternoon," Frankie addressed the sea of feminine faces regarding her with frank curiosity. Or was it still morning in California? After all, she was on Pacific Standard Time now. A fine first impression that would make, if her future housemates thought she couldn't even tell time! "I'm Frances Foster. I'd like to see somebody about a room."

A pert, freckle-faced redhead jerked a thumb in the direction of a carved double door at one end of the room. "You want to see Miss Williams, the directress. Through those doors and to your left. You can't miss it."

"Thank you."

For the next few seconds, there was no sound but the clicking of Frankie's high-heeled shoes on the tile floor. Just as the double doors closed behind her, a voice said in an audible whisper, "Maybe she'd better see someone about voice lessons while she's at it. Did you ever *hear* such an accent?"

Thankfully, the resulting blow to Frankie's confidence was short-lived. In spite of her formidable title, Miss Williams proved to be a motherly woman with stylishly coiffed graying hair and a twinkle in her eye. By the time Frankie re-emerged through the double doors some ten minutes later, she was the proud possessor of a room (well, half a room, really, since she would be sharing it with one of the other girls) at the bargain price of only fifteen dollars a week—more expensive than housing in Georgia, perhaps, but quite reasonable by Hollywood standards, and besides, it included two hot meals a day. Of course, the rules for residence were rather stringent, but since Frankie didn't smoke or drink and had no intention of entertaining gentleman callers in her room, she didn't think compliance would be overly taxing.

The sight that met her eyes when she reached the foyer was enough to wipe the self-satisfied smile from her face. Mitch had dumped her suitcases just inside the door and now stood flexing his muscles for a gaggle of admiring females who "oohed" and "aahed" and vied for the privilege of squeezing his bulging biceps.

"Where did you say you played football?" one girl cooed. "UCLA?"

"Texas A & M," Mitch corrected her.

"I have to attend a wrap party tomorrow night, and I don't have a date," purred a voluptuous brunette. "Would you like to escort me?"

"I'd only embarrass you," Mitch demurred. "I don't have a tuxedo."

"Rent one at Brooks Brothers. You can pick me up at eight."

"Ahem!" Frankie tapped her toes against the hardwood

floor.

Mitch started guiltily and picked up her suitcases. "Here, let me get that for you."

"No men are allowed beyond the first floor. So I guess this is goodbye."

Frankie dropped the smaller of her two cases and held out her gloved hand. Mitch took it, but instead of the firm handshake she'd intended he gave her fingers a squeeze, making the gesture unexpectedly intimate. "Maybe not. After all, I know where to find you."

"Here, I'll help," said the freckle-faced redhead, picking up Frankie's case. "What room are you in?"

Frankie waited until they were halfway up the stairs, then asked, "Who was that—that *female*?"

"The one who tried to vamp your boyfriend?"

"He's not my—"

"Her name is Pauline Moore, but we all call her Theda Baracuda behind her back."

Frankie choked back a giggle. Her mother had seen the notorious Theda Bara in *Cleopatra* years ago, before Frankie was born. Mama had never forgotten it; in fact, that old silent film was responsible for her conviction that going to Hollywood was a girl's first step on the road to hell.

"Yes sir, Pauline is the Studio Club's own Will Rogers: she

never met a man she didn't like. By the way, everybody calls me Roxie, but my professional name is Roxanne Carr. Roxanne Carr, the Movie Star. Has a nice ring to it, don't you think?"

Roxie paused before a closed door and tapped on the frame. "Knock, knock, anybody home?"

Receiving no reply, she turned the knob and, finding the door unlocked, pushed it open and snapped on the overhead light. Frankie found herself standing at the threshold of a small but well-proportioned room sparsely yet tastefully decorated in blue and white gingham and floral prints. The only fault to be found was the white framed twin beds, one of whose mattresses possessed a lump of remarkable size. Even as she focused on this flaw, the lump stirred and a flush-cheeked girl sat up, clutching the covers to her pajama-clad chest.

"Sorry, Kathleen, I didn't know you were still in bed," said Roxie, apparently unfazed by the discovery. "Hot date last night?"

"No, just not feeling well." Kathleen raked her fingers through a fringe of blond curls worn like Norma Shearer's in *Juliet.*

"Still? That's, what, three days in a row. Maybe you'd better see a doctor."

Kathleen shrugged. "Maybe."

"I've brought you a new roommate," Roxie said, dumping

Frankie's suitcase on the floor beside a mirrored dresser. "Kathleen Stuart, meet—?"

"Frances," Frankie put in hastily. "Frances Foster, but my friends call me Frankie. Gosh, I'm sorry to disturb you like this."

"No trouble," Kathleen assured her, throwing back the covers. "I should have been up hours ago. I have a casting call first thing tomorrow."

"That's right, you're reading for a part in *The Virgin Queen*, aren't you?"

Kathleen nodded. "Gwyneth, lady in waiting to Queen Elizabeth. It's a costume picture," she added unnecessarily, for Frankie's benefit. "Not a very big role, but the kind that could get me noticed if I do a good job with it."

Roxie kicked off her shoes and perched on the foot of the bed, patting the mattress as an invitation for Frankie to join her. "I hope you get the part," she told Kathleen with a malicious gleam in her eye. "That would be one in the eye for Pauline!"

"Pauline is awfully good," Kathleen said in the other girl's defense. "Remember, she had a part in the last Clark Gable film."

"As if she'd ever let us forget it! Two seconds on screen as a hat check girl!" Roxie made a derisive sound Mama would have called a snort. "I hope her scene ends up on the cutting room floor. It would serve her right!"

"She'd only get others," Kathleen said, not without sympathy.

Roxie sighed. "You're right, of course."

Kathleen turned to Frankie. "None of us are very fond of Pauline, but she does get more work than any of us."

"And no wonder!" Roxie cast a furtive glance back at the half-open door and lowered her voice to a conspiratorial whisper. "They say she gives her best performances on her back."

"On her back?" Frankie echoed, baffled by this seeming impossibility. "But she would have to be lying—oh!" She blushed crimson at the implication.

"Not that she's the only one, not by a long shot," Roxie continued. "Lots of girls figure it's the fastest way out of Central Casting and into a studio contract."

Frankie shook her head. "Not me. I could never do such a thing!"

"Never say 'never,' " cautioned Kathleen, suddenly solemn. "When the perfect role comes along, some girls figure it's worth any price. After all, you may not get another shot at stardom. You do what you have to do, or you go home a failure."

Or you throw yourself headfirst from the Hollywoodland sign, like poor Peg Entwhistle had done a few years back. Either way, Frankie couldn't imagine any role worth such desperate measures. Still, she didn't want to quarrel with her new friends, so she was relieved, if a bit bewildered, when Roxie steered the conversation in a new direction.

"So, have you registered with Central Casting yet?"

"I don't think so," Frankie said doubtfully.

Roxie laughed. "If you don't know, then you haven't done it."

"Central Casting is the office the studios call when they need to hire extras," Kathleen explained. "They're small parts, usually non-speaking, but at least you get acting experience."

Frankie tried hard not to let her disappointment show. "I'd hoped to get a contract with one of the big studios."

Roxie let out a bark of somewhat bitter laughter. "Don't we all! Unfortunately, every female in Hollywood has the same thing in mind. Working as an extra may not be glamorous, but it pays the rent. Besides, there's always the chance you might catch the eye of someone important."

"But—"

"It's easy to register," Kathleen added, apparently seeing nothing wrong with this plan for Frankie's future. "All you have to do is go to the Central Casting office and fill out a form. If you have a recent photograph of yourself, leave it with them. If not, it's worth the expense of having one professionally made."

34

Photographs, or a lack thereof, were no problem. Mama had taken her to have her photo taken in the full-skirted white chiffon gown Frankie had worn to her debutante ball. She'd worn her grandmother's pearl earrings, and her hair was pinned up in a sophisticated style. In fact, she'd looked every inch the Hollywood starlet she still hoped to be. But she was reluctant to add her own likeness to the hundreds of anonymous photos at Central Casting without first trying her luck at the major studios. And so the following morning, dressed in a cream-colored linen suit and armed with a map and a bus schedule, she set out to storm the citadel.

Her first stop was Columbia Pictures, where the receptionist hardly even looked at her. "We get most of our extras through Central Casting," she said in the world-weary accents of one who had made the same speech more times than she could count. "Fill out a registration card with them, and if anything comes up, we'll let you know."

"Can't I at least leave my photograph for the casting director?"

The receptionist smiled regretfully and shook her head. "I'm afraid it would only get lost in all the clutter."

Since Frankie could see her own reflection on the surface of the pristine desk, she understood this excuse as the dismissal it was clearly intended to be. She thanked the receptionist politely—Mama's daughter would do nothing less—but knew better than to hold her breath.

From Columbia she went to MGM and from MGM to Paramount, with no greater success. She dug a bit deeper into her purse for bus fare and ventured farther afield to Universal and Twentieth Century-Fox, but the story was always the same.

"Don't call us," one industry insider recommended, taking Frankie firmly by the elbow and all but frog-marching her to the door. "We'll call you."

Her last stop, at Monumental Pictures, proved even more fruitless than all the rest. At least at the other studios a real person had spoken to her, however unpromisingly. At Monumental, however, the reception room stood vacant, without so much as a cold coffee cup on the desk to suggest that it had ever been inhabited at all.

"Hello?" called Frankie, undaunted. "Is anyone there?"

Receiving no reply, she ventured past the desk and into the hallway. She could hear the faint sounds of voices further down the corridor, and she started in their direction, the thick carpet beneath her feet absorbing the sound of her footsteps. At the end of the hall was a half-open door bearing a brass nameplate reading "Arthur Cohen, Executive Producer." As she drew nearer, the voices within began to resolve themselves into words—angry words. A previously unsuspected instinct for self-preservation warned her against announcing her presence.

"Damn it, Artie, this is the opportunity of a lifetime!"

The unseen Artie, presumably Mr. Arthur Cohen himself, gave a derisive snort. "Opportunity to go bankrupt, more like. Have you heard what the Mitchell dame and her agent are asking? A hundred grand!"

"Since when does anybody pay the asking price? Make 'em a counter offer, and see what happens."

"I know what'll happen. Either they'll turn it down, and I'm no better off than I was before, or they'll accept it—and I'm a hell of a lot worse."

The first speaker's response was drowned out by a metallic ringing like a spoon against the cup. A moment later a not unpleasant odor of herbs and almonds filled the air, tickling Frankie's nose.

"Mayer says no Civil War picture ever made a nickel," Artie said once the stirring sound had stopped. "You think you suddenly know more about making pictures than Louis B. Mayer?"

Frankie gasped. They were talking about *Gone with the Wind*! The whole country was hoping for a film version of Margaret Mitchell's novel, even (maybe especially) those who hadn't yet read the thousand-page brick of a book. Forgetting for the moment the hostility with which the issue was being debated, Frankie pictured herself in ruffled hoop skirts, lifting her tear-stained face to the camera and declaring that "Tomorrow is another day." Then Artie's companion spoke again, more clearly now, dragging her away from Tara and back to reality.

"—big Technicolor production, like I wanted to do with *The Virgin Queen.*"

"I keep telling you, Technicolor is nothing but a fad—and a damned expensive one at that."

"You said the same thing ten years ago about the talkies. If it had been left up to you we'd still be making the old silent flicks."

Artie took exception to this accusation, slamming his fist into something—the wall, perhaps, or the top of his desk. "God knows one of us has to show some restraint! 'Technicolor,' my Aunt Fanny! Give me a good old black and white horror flick any day. That's what the public wants—some sweet young thing in a see-through nightie tiptoeing down the stairs with a candle in her hand—"

"And you were the master of the genre, Artie, no one's arguing with that," his companion assured him in conciliatory tones. "But that kind of thing is box office poison these days, thanks to the Hays Office."

Artie's bluntly stated opinion of the Hays Office and its

censoring practices caused Frankie to clap one hand over her open mouth.

"I'm inclined to agree with you, but it looks like they're here to stay, and there's nothing we can do about it. Look, if you're not happy with the way the industry is headed, maybe it's time you got out, pursued some other interests. I'd be willing to buy you out—"

"With what?" scoffed Artie. "You don't have a dime you didn't make in the business."

"And what money do *you* have that you didn't marry?"

"You leave my wife out of this!"

"But the business—"

"Yeah, the business—the business *I* started with two old cameras in an empty barn while you were off at some fancy-pants college getting yourself educated! No, if we break up the partnership, you'll be the one to leave, not me. You want me out, you'll have to kill me first."

Frankie had heard enough. Groping for the wall with one shaking hand, she took a backward step, then another. She had almost reached the foyer when her hand struck a framed movie poster hanging on the wall, setting it swinging back and forth on its nail.

"What the hell was that?" Artie demanded.

Frankie didn't know if they would come after her, and

didn't wait to find out. She spun on her heel and bolted from the studio as if the devil himself were at her heels. She didn't stop running until she reached the curb, waving wildly for an approaching taxi.

Thanks to a traffic accident at the corner of Sunset and Camden, it was almost seven o'clock by the time the taxi delivered her to the Studio Club. By that time, her panic had faded, and she felt a bit foolish for her precipitous departure. There was probably a perfectly logical, perfectly innocent explanation for the conversation she'd overheard. By overreacting, she had thrown away her best chance to meet someone high enough on the corporate ladder to give her a job. True, neither one of them had sounded as if he would have been in the mood to do anyone any favors, but surely she could have coaxed them round.

Now it was too late, and all she had to show for her day's efforts was a fifty-cent taxi fare. She felt hot, tired, and sweaty. Her suit of cream colored linen, so stylish just that morning, was now lined with creases, and what remained of the makeup she had so carefully applied that morning was now streaked and shiny. Given the way her day had gone so far, it hardly seemed surprising when she walked into the foyer of the Studio Club and saw a good-looking young man in a black tuxedo. His hair was slicked back with brilliantine, and under his arm he carried a cardboard florist's box. Frankie's hand rose instinctively to smooth her hair, but even as she made the unconscious gesture, she realized there was something vaguely familiar about the young man. The clothes were certainly different, and the liberal application of brilliantine made his sandy hair appear darker, but the snub nose and the faintly mocking blue eyes were the same.

"Mitch?" She took an involuntary step in his direction. "What are you doing here?"

Something about his grin, or maybe it was just his formal attire, made her feel more disheveled than ever. "Picking up my date. We're going to the Cocoanut Grove."

Frankie stiffened. "I don't remember saying I'd go to the Cocoanut Grove with you!"

"I don't remember asking you. Ah, there's my date now!"

His gaze shifted to the staircase beyond. Turning, Frankie beheld Pauline Moore descending the stairs in a slinky black number whose plunging neckline made the most of her considerable assets. As she glided across the foyer, Frankie saw that the back of the gown dipped almost to her waist. Frankie didn't see how anyone could possibly wear a brassiere under such a gown and suspected Pauline hadn't tried very hard to find a way. Still, she couldn't deny that Pauline looked every inch a movie star. Her dark hair dipped dramatically over one eye, and her penciled eyebrows and crimson lips could have come from the hand of Mr. Max Factor himself. Frankie didn't know why Pauline had bothered; given the view from both front and back, no man in the joint would be looking at her face, anyway.

"I hope I haven't kept you waiting too long," Pauline purred.

"Even if you did, the results are worth every minute," Mitch assured her.

"Oh, and you brought me flowers. How sweet! Will you pin them on for me?"

Frankie, unwilling witness to this process, thought it took a ridiculous length of time for him to affix the corsage to Pauline's bosom. At last the operation was complete. Mitch took the fur wrap Pauline carried over her arm and draped it over her shoulders.

" 'Night, Frances," Mitch told her. "I'd ask you to come along, but you know what they say about three being a crowd."

Frankie raised her gloved hand to her mouth and faked a yawn. "How sweet of you to think of me!" she said in her best Pauline imitation. "But I couldn't possibly go anywhere tonight except to the bath and then straight to bed. I'm exhausted! I just got back from a late interview with Mr. Arthur Cohen. Maybe you've heard of him? Monumental Pictures? But I mustn't keep you standing here! Ta-ta, Pauline, don't let Mitch keep you out too late. We girls need our beauty sleep, you know."

Frankie kept smiling and waving until the door closed behind them, then collapsed onto one of the wicker chairs, reluctant to go upstairs to her room. She had no desire to make small talk with a roommate who was still essentially a stranger. She felt lower than she'd ever felt in all her life. Georgia was hundreds of miles away, her money was almost gone, she hadn't yet met with a single Hollywood big shot, and now her only friend—no, make that *acquaintance*—was going out to dinner with a half-naked floozy. Oh, the glamorous life of an actress!

3

Gentlemen's Agreement (1947)
Directed by Elia Kazan
Starring Gregory Peck and Dorothy McGuire

If Mitch suspected Pauline Moore of having a romantic interest in him, he was disabused of this notion within half an hour of their arrival at the Cocoanut Grove. He'd been lucky enough to score a table for two at the edge of the dance floor, but after they'd glided across the floor to the orchestra's rendition of "Begin the Beguine," it appeared that Pauline had lost her taste for his company. He watched as she flitted about the perimeter of a boisterous table on the opposite side of the room, now laughing animatedly as a portly middle-aged man stole an arm about her waist, now sipping from a glass of something that was definitely *not* the ginger ale she'd asked Mitch to order for her.

Mitch wasn't offended; heaven knew he'd gone on plenty

of dates with less than pure motives himself. In a way, it was fascinating to watch an expert at work. He leaned back in his chair and gestured to a pretty cigarette girl in a short frilly skirt and high heels. She was probably an actress; if there was one thing Mitch had learned since getting off the train in Pasadena, it was that every passably good-looking female between fifteen and forty was an actress.

He bought one of her cigarettes for a nickel and lit it from the candle in the center of the table. Then he leaned back in his chair and blew smoke rings while he watched the show unfolding across the room. The older man's hand had abandoned Pauline's waist and crept upward to caress her bare back. If Pauline objected to his advances, she gave no sign of it. Mitch tried to imagine a certain Georgia peach allowing old men to paw her for the sake of a few seconds on the silver screen, and his eyebrows drew together in the fierce scowl that opposing linemen had once found so intimidating.

"Hey, pal, what's eating you?" The youngish man leaning against Pauline's abandoned chair wasn't handsome enough to be an actor, but he seemed at home amongst the Hollywood crowd. "Artie Cohen beating your time with the lady? Or maybe she's beating your time with him?"

Mitch bristled at the imagined slight to his manhood, until he realized that his companion had taken him for an out-of-work actor looking for his big break. He wondered fleetingly how a fellow hoping to be "discovered" might approach a producer, but quickly banished the thought. Considering the ladies' tactics, he wasn't sure he wanted to know.

"Not me." He shook his head and gestured for the other man to sit down. "I'm an engineer, not an actor."

"Engineer? No kidding?"

"A & M, class of '35."

The newcomer eyed Mitch appraisingly. "Know anything about electricity?"

Mitch shrugged. "I took a couple of courses in college." He'd also disconnected the alarm on the dormitory door so he and his teammates could break curfew without fear of detection, but this hardly seemed the time to mention it.

"Cohen brothers are looking to hire a new best boy over at Monumental. Interested?"

"Depends," said Mitch. "What's a best boy?"

"Assistant to the gaffer—chief lighting technician. Might give you a chance to keep an eye on that skirt of yours." He jerked his head toward Pauline, who was now perched on Arthur Cohen's lap.

"Hmm." Mitch pondered the possibilities, but keeping an eye on Pauline was not uppermost among them. "Would a— what did you call him? Best boy?—be in a position to help a friend get a job as an extra?"

"Hey, we're talking about an assistant electrician, not an executive producer. Still, the suits are getting antsy. *The Virgin Queen* should already be in the can by now, but the leading lady hasn't even been cast yet. Say, how would your friend look swishing around the set in a farthingale?"

Mitch tried to picture Frankie in the stiff brocade skirts of the Elizabethan era, and chuckled. "I dunno. Might be good for a laugh."

"That's no good, then. It's a swashbuckling costume piece, not a comedy. Still, it couldn't hurt to bring her along. Who knows? Maybe the big guy will take a liking to her."

Mitch glanced at the table across the room, where Arthur Cohen's pudgy hand cupped Pauline's shapely rear. "Maybe," he said doubtfully.

"That must have been some party last night," Frankie remarked, staring fixedly out the window of the secondhand roadster at the passing scenery. "I never even heard Pauline come in."

"She may not have, for all I know," Mitch answered, making his turn onto Sunset Boulevard. "Come in, I mean."

"You mean you don't know? Mitch, don't tell me you just left her there!"

"Don't blame me. She got a better offer."

"Oh." Frankie frowned over this revelation, reluctant to think ill of the most successful of her housemates. "Mama always says a girl should dance with the one who brought her."

"Believe me, their minds weren't on dancing."

"Maybe she just wasn't brought up right," continued Frankie, struggling to be charitable. "Maybe she was never taught any better, and she's a bit slow, socially."

Mitch gave a bark of laughter, which he turned rather unconvincingly into a cough. " 'Slow' is the *last* word I would use to describe Pauline!"

"I know she's awfully pretty, and all the boys seem to go ga-ga over her, but doesn't it ever occur to any of you that Pauline just doesn't seem to be very *nice*?"

"I think probably a few guys have figured it out," Mitch observed cryptically. "I'll bet most of them consider it a big part of her charm."

Frankie nodded in understanding. "You mean they want to reform her, or something."

"Or something." Mitch swerved to avoid a milk truck parked along the street.

Frankie cocked her head, regarding him curiously. "You don't seem awfully upset about it."

He shrugged. "I wasn't all that keen on her—didn't even

know her that well, really. Remember, *she's* the one who asked *me* to escort her. Besides, if I'd been tripping the light fantastic with Pauline, I wouldn't have the inside track on a job at Monumental Pictures."

Frankie's stomach flip-flopped at the mention of the studio where she'd had such a scare less than twenty-four hours earlier. But as Mitch wheeled the car into the drive, her fears faded. The Spanish revival stucco building looked just as it had before, but today its arched portico and red clay tile roof suggested nothing more sinister than stylish prosperity. Mitch exchanged a word or two with the guard at the gate, and a moment later they were inside.

Today a receptionist sat behind the front desk, a middle-aged woman with horn-rimmed glasses perched on the end of her nose.

"Mitchell Gannon and Frances Foster, here to see Mr. Cohen," Mitch informed her, giving her his most disarming smile.

She pursed her lips. "Which Mr. Cohen, sir?"

Mitch hesitated only a moment. "Artie—er, Mr. Arthur Cohen, if you please."

Apparently the receptionist did *not* please. "Do you have an appointment?"

"No, but I believe Mr. Cohen is expecting me." Mitch

glanced pointedly toward the shiny black telephone on her desk. "Why don't we ask him?"

With a disdainful sniff, she lifted the receiver from its cradle and dialed a number with unnecessary force. "Mr. Cohen, there's a young man here by the name of Gannon who claims you're expecting him."

There was a pause during which Frankie and Mitch could hear the buzz of a masculine voice at the other end of the line, although the words were indistinguishable.

"Gannon. Yes, that's right. Mitchell Gannon." Another pause. "Yes sir, I'll show him in."

She replaced the receiver. "He says he can give you fifteen minutes," she allowed grudgingly. "If you'll follow me, please."

As she emerged from behind the desk, Mitch took Frankie's arm and fell in behind. "Charming woman," he murmured in Frankie's ear.

Frankie made no reply. She was retracing the steps she'd taken two days ago, down the same carpeted corridor lined with framed posters of previous Monumental films. She wondered which one she had knocked askew during her undignified exit. It was impossible to tell now, since it had apparently been straightened.

A moment later, the receptionist flung open the door, and Frankie had her first glimpse of Hollywood magnate Arthur

Cohen. In fact, he wasn't much to look at. He was at least fifty years old—ancient, in Frankie's eyes—and his receding hair was slicked over his bald spot with brilliantine. When he rose to greet them, she saw he wasn't much taller than her own five feet four inches. His lack of stature, along with the gold watch chain stretching across his bulging middle, gave the impression of a man almost as broad as he was tall. And yet there was something strangely compelling about the man, something that went beyond his pin-striped suit and the massive gold rings weighing down his fingers.

"Mitchell Gannon and Frances Foster," the receptionist informed her boss, then backed away, closing the door behind her.

"Come in, come in," Arthur Cohen said jovially, gesturing toward the two leather upholstered chairs positioned before his desk. "I believe you're an engineering student?"

"Graduate, sir. Texas A & M, class of '35."

"Electrical engineering, you say?"

Mitch shook his head. "Not my specialty, but I've had a few courses."

"And your specialty?"

"Civil engineering. I was on my way to Nevada and the Boulder Dam when I had a sudden change of plans." He glanced at Frankie. "I guess you could say I was bitten by the movie bug."

Mr. Cohen's belly shook as he laughed aloud. "You'll find plenty of fellow sufferers in this town, my boy. It happens to us all. But you do realize," he added, growing suddenly serious, "however flattering the job title may sound, 'best boy' is little more than an assistant electrician. I like you, kid, but I'm afraid you're overqualified."

Mitch leaned back in his chair. "I'm not afraid of working my way up, sir. During my four years at A & M, I went from fourth string lineman to second team All-American."

"I'm afraid I never cared much for football," the older man admitted, shaking his head. "Horseracing is more to my liking, and one thing it's taught me is that sometimes it's smart to put your money on a dark horse. I can give you thirty dollars a week to start, with more to come if you show a knack for the business."

"Thank you, sir. And Miss Foster?"

Mr. Cohen studied Frankie for a long moment. "She's an ingénue," he pronounced at last. "The trouble with ingénues is that it's all or nothing with them. Either they fall apart at the idea of kissing a man for the cameras and look stiff as a board on film, or else they lose it to the first pretty-boy actor to cross their path, and then three months later they find themselves in trouble and come crying for the studio to fix it. I'm sorry,

Miss—Farmer, was it?"

"Foster," said Frankie, crestfallen. "But I—"

"—But I'll have to pass," concluded Mr. Cohen in a voice that brooked no argument.

"If you'll give her a try, sir, I'll vouch for her good behavior," Mitch promised, raising one hand Boy Scout style.

Frankie was not exactly sure what it was that Mr. Cohen thought she might do, but she was highly indignant at the idea that Mitch—who smoked and gambled and ran around with fast women—should be hired while she was not. She opened her mouth to protest such an injustice, but before she could utter a word, Mitch kicked her in the shins. She bit her lip to keep from crying out.

"Well—" Arthur Cohen picked up a fountain pen and twiddled it between his fingers.

"If she doesn't find work soon, I'll have to turn down your offer and take Cousin Frances back to Georgia," Mitch continued. "I promised Aunt Beulah I'd look after her."

Frankie added lying to the catalog of his sins.

"I won't promise her a contract, but maybe there's some work available for her as an extra." He slapped the pen down on the desk. "We'll be shooting exteriors tomorrow on the back lot. Be there at seven o'clock, both of you." Turning to Frankie, he added, "Tell the CD I said to work you into a crowd scene or two."

"Yes, sir! Thank you, sir!" Frankie took his hand in both of hers and shook it vigorously. "You won't regret it, I promise."

Mitch made his own more restrained goodbyes, and he and Frankie soon filed past the receptionist (who squirreled away a well-worn copy of *Photoplay* at their approach) and out into the blinding brilliance of the spring sun.

"I can hardly believe it!" Frankie exclaimed, flinging her arms wide. "At this time tomorrow, we'll both be working in the movies!"

Mitch regarded her enthusiasm with one ironically arched eyebrow. "You're welcome."

"Of course I appreciate what you did for me," Frankie said hastily, returning to earth with a thud. "Still, I would have been even more grateful if you could have managed it without kicking me in the shins. You probably ruined my last pair of stockings, to say nothing of leaving a nasty bruise."

She lifted her skirt to the knee to survey the damage, wholly ignorant of the fact that twelve inches of shapely, silk-clad calf had the power to fire Mitch's imagination in a way that Pauline Moore's elegant overexposure had not.

Mitch sighed and looked resolutely away. It wasn't his "cousin's" good behavior he was worried about.

It was his own.

4

There's No Business Like Show Business (1954)
Directed by Walter Lang
Starring Ethel Merman, Mitzi Gaynor, Dan Dailey, Donald
O'Connor and Marilyn Monroe

Frankie arose before dawn the next morning, eager to begin her career as an actress. She knew working as an extra was unlikely to be very glamorous, but then, Frankie had no intention of remaining an extra, so she was determined to look as glamorous as possible. Unfortunately, she was obliged to perform this minor miracle in the dark so as not to wake up Kathleen, still buried beneath the covers of the other twin bed. With this admirable goal in mind, Frankie groped her way to the dresser in search of the new padded brassiere designed to make the most of her modest assets. She sat down on the edge of the bed to slip on her silk stockings, snapping the garters to hold them in place and then feeling the backs of her legs to make sure the seams were straight. Finally, she threw a floral print dress over head, smoothing the trumpet-shaped skirt over her hips before snatching up her stack-heeled shoes and tiptoeing from the room in her stocking feet.

A line had already formed outside the bathroom at the end of the hall; apparently Frankie was not the only one at the Studio Club who hoped to find work that day.

"Pauline's in there," Roxie said, jerking her thumb in the direction of the closed door. "We'll be lucky if she's out before lunch."

This was an exaggeration, of course; a mere half hour passed before the door flew open and Pauline sailed out, stunning as always in a crimson Elsa Schiaparelli suit. Roxie ducked in behind her, promising to hurry, and, true to her word, was out in five minutes, leaving Frankie in sole possession of the bathroom.

After performing the mundane tasks of brushing her teeth and washing her face, Frankie arranged her brown hair in rows of S-shaped waves, then applied cosmetics in just the right amount to enhance her complexion without making her look "fast." Remembering Mama's admonitions, she tiptoed back into her room to fetch a pair of short white gloves and a wide-brimmed picture hat before going downstairs to call for a taxi.

Mitch had offered to pick her up, and a quick consultation with her handbag—much lighter now than it had been when she had left Atlanta—almost made her wish she had taken him up on the offer. Still, she was uncomfortably aware that she stood in his debt already. It was bad enough that she should have him to thank for landing her first job, without also having to depend on him to deliver her to the set.

At last the taxi drew up beside the curb.

"Monumental Pictures," Frankie told the driver as she climbed into the back seat. "And can you hurry? I'm running a little late."

She soon lived to regret this request. The driver, taking her at her word, floored the pedal and swerved out into the traffic with tires squealing. Palm trees and power lines passed by in a blur, and by the time the cab slammed to a stop at the front gate, Frankie's face was as white as her knuckles.

"You'll have to get out here, sister," the cabbie informed her. "Security guard won't let me through."

Frankie followed the direction of his gaze and saw a uniformed security guard observing their arrival from a glass-enclosed booth. Had he not been isolated in this manner, she might have fallen on his neck in gratitude. Instead, she paid her fare and exited the cab on wobbly legs. As the cabbie drove away, she approached the guard in his booth.

"Good morning, I'm Frances Foster. Can you tell me how to get to the back lot?"

He jerked his thumb in the direction of the road beyond the gate, then added as a caveat, "Before I let you in, though, I'll have to ask you to state your business."

Frankie lifted her chin in a gesture half confident, half defiant. "I'm going to be working as an extra. Mr. Cohen himself told me to report to the back lot."

At the mention of the producer's name, the gates swung open as if by magic. "In you go, then, Miss Foster, and good luck to you."

"Thank you. I'm sure I'll need it," she confessed sheepishly. "It's my first real acting job, you know."

"I never would have guessed it," declared the guard with less than perfect truth. "It's quite a walk to the back lot, though. I could call a studio taxi for you—"

"No, no, that's quite all right." Frankie had had her fill of taxi rides for one day. "I don't mind walking, really."

She set out down the main road into the heart of the studio, even though she had only the vaguest idea where she was going. Beyond the Spanish adobe and clay tiles of the front building, the architecture was strictly utilitarian. In truth, Frankie found it a bit disappointing; the large windowless white buildings marked "Soundstage A" and "Soundstage B" looked more like warehouses than the sort of place where one might expect to see movie magic being created.

The studio property was larger than Frankie had expected, and the morning sun was beginning to grow warm. She began to wish she'd worn shoes with lower heels. One or two cars passed by, and a few pedestrians cast curious glances in her direction, but no one offered her a ride, much less a job. She was beginning to wonder if she would even recognize the back lot if she saw it when she rounded the corner of yet another nondescript white building and gasped in amazement. A Wild West streetscape rubbed shoulders with an exotic tropical village, which abutted a modern American residential suburb. In the distance rose the ruddy brick towers of an ancient Tudor castle. Dozens of people milled around it, all dressed in the stiff brocade skirts and starched neck ruffs of Elizabethan England.

For a long moment, Frankie just stood there staring in awe. Eventually, however, her aching feet demanded that she take action. As she drew nearer, she realized her first impressions had not been entirely accurate. Queen Elizabeth's castle, she was disappointed to discover, was nothing more than a backdrop of plywood painted to resemble bricks. As for the Elizabethan hordes, not only were they talking twentieth-century slang to each other in distinctly American accents, there were also scattered amongst them a number of people wearing modern street clothes.

The foremost of these appeared to be a man seated apart from all the rest in a canvas folding chair, who surveyed the scene with a critical eye and occasionally barked out commands through a megaphone. Frankie started in his direction, but was waylaid by a good-looking young man in a blue and scarlet doublet and hose.

"Sorry, miss, but it's a closed set," he said, his smile taking the sting from his words. "No visitors allowed."

Frankie responded with a smile of her own. "Oh, I wouldn't think of intruding! But I need to speak to the person in charge of casting extras. Mr. Cohen wants him to give me a role."

In fact, Mr. Cohen had promised nothing beyond an anonymous spot in a crowd scene, but, as Frankie's father had occasionally pontificated over dinner, the difference between truth and falsehood was often no more than a matter of degrees.

"So you're Artie's latest discovery, eh?"

It seemed to Frankie that the young man's smile, which had appeared so open and friendly, now seemed a bit knowing, and his admiring gaze had grown, if no less admiring, certainly more calculating. Frankie resented the suggestion—which had certainly been implied, although not directly stated—that Mr. Cohen's interest in her was somehow amorous in nature. Still, it was even more galling to admit that she owed her big break to a chance-met stranger on a train. She gritted her teeth and forced a smile.

"If you'll just point me in the direction of the casting director—"

"Oh, right! You'll want Mr. Harrison. Over there, in the checkered lid."

Frankie trained her gaze in the direction he indicated and finally identified a short, wiry man dressed in gray plus-fours, a v-necked sweater vest over rolled-up shirt sleeves, and a soft plaid cap. She thanked her medieval swain, and set out in pursuit of her new quarry.

"Artie sent you, eh?" observed Harrison, after hearing her story. "Well, looks like you're in luck. We'll be shooting the tavern scene after lunch, and one of the serving wenches is out sick. Go to the costume trailer—the one on the end, there—and see what they can do for you."

"Oh, thank you, Mr. Harrison!" Frankie seized his hand and pumped it vigorously. "You won't regret it, I promise! I'll be the best serving wench you've ever seen, cross my heart!"

"Tavern wench, eh?" The costume woman, on her knees making last-minute adjustments to someone's hem, muttered around a mouthful of pins. "Gimme a sec, and I'll see what I can do."

The woman made a few stitches, then broke off the thread with her teeth. "There you go, Alice, but try not to get your skirt caught in those heels. Sheesh! Whoever heard of a medieval maiden in high heels?"

"I'm not medieval, I'm Elizabethan," Alice retorted as she opened the trailer door and tottered down the steps. "Besides, I *need* the high heels, remember? Mr. Cohen wants me to be tall enough that William can bend down and kiss me without falling off his horse."

"Well, that's done, anyway," the costume mistress pronounced, rising to her feet and studying Frankie with a critical eye. "How do you do? You can call me Rose. And you are?"

"Frank—Frances," Frankie said. "Frances Foster."

"So, Frances Foster, we're supposed to turn you into a serving wench, are we? Let's see if your hair is long enough to do without a wig."

Before Frankie knew what was happening, Rose had seized a brush and yanked out all the curls she had so carefully styled. But this was the least of the indignities she was obliged to endure for the sake of stardom. By the time she beheld her reflection in the mirror a half-hour later, her own mother would not have recognized her—or, worse, would have fallen over in a faint if she had. Gone was the demure floral frock, replaced by a long brown skirt and a full white blouse topped with a laced bodice that pushed Frankie's previously unremarkable bosom upward and outward.

Frankie, observing this unexpected development with equal parts mortification and awe, protested feebly, "I can't go out there looking like this!"

Rose had already turned away and was engaged in putting away the tools of her trade, but at Frankie's outburst she looked back. "If you want to make it in show biz, honey, you can and will." Seeing the young actress was not convinced, she added, "Most of the guys out there were here before the Hays Code. They've seen a lot worse, believe me."

Modesty warred with ambition as Frankie pirouetted to and fro in front of the mirror, studying her reflection with a critical eye. Mama would be shocked at the expanse of bare white bosom exposed above the scooped neckline of her blouse; still, there was something about the costume that projected a certain earthy allure that her demure white debutante gown had utterly failed to capture. Besides, in this costume she actually *looked* like an actress; if she only intended to accept roles in which she would look and dress exactly like Frances Foster, Georgia belle, she might as well have stayed home. Someday she would laugh as she told the *Variety* reporter all about how she got her start as a serving wench in *The Virgin Queen*. Her mind made up, Frankie squared her shoulders (an act which did nothing to detract from the startling effect of her costume), opened the door, and stepped out of the trailer and into her new career.

Just as Rose had predicted, no one seemed to notice her décolletage, or even pay much attention to her at all; everyone's efforts seemed to be focused on the task of hoisting a farthingale-clad woman atop a prancing white horse.

"Is that Queen Elizabeth?" Frankie asked a fellow serving wench.

"No, it's her stunt double. Can't risk a big star's safety by putting her on a skittish horse. Matter of fact, Queen Elizabeth hasn't even been cast yet, and production is way behind schedule. So we shoot the scenes we can, and save the queen's close-ups for last."

Frankie knew from reading *Variety* magazine that scenes were not shot in chronological order. On a practical level, this meant Frankie had no idea what the plot of the movie was about and could bring nothing to her role more creative than mindless obedience. When the time came to film the crowd scene outside the castle, Frankie was herded with the other extras into the wide open area in front of the massive façade. Here they were instructed to wave their arms in the air and shout "rhubarb,

rhubarb" to simulate crowd noise while Queen Elizabeth (or her stunt double) and her entourage rode through on their caparisoned horses.

"Why 'rhubarb?' " Frankie asked the elderly village woman standing next to her.

The woman shrugged her homespun-clad shoulders. "Why not? It doesn't really matter what you say, as long as the words can't be understood. Over at Paramount they use 'carrots and peas,' while at Columbia it's 'watermelon cantaloupe.' I don't know why it always seems to be food; maybe everyone's just thinking about lunch."

Occasionally Frankie caught a glimpse of Arthur Cohen standing on the edge of the carefully orchestrated chaos, sometimes beaming with paternal pride, sometimes scowling in displeasure. Unfortunately, it was necessary to shoot the scene several times, with long delays in between, during which an unglamorous but invaluable crew member called a "grip" hosed down the cloud of dust raised by the horses' hooves, while another less fortunate grip was given the unenviable task of shoveling horse manure from the set.

By the time the cast and crew finally broke for lunch, Frankie's arms ached from waving, and her voice was hoarse from shouting enthusiastic vegetable greetings to the fake queen. She joined the throng of cast and crew heading for the commissary, and soon discovered one of the less pleasant realities of Hollywood: extras ate last. The stars, of course, had dismounted their horses as soon as filming was completed, and were whisked away from the back lot in studio cars. Frankie hadn't expected to join their number, but she hadn't thought to be outranked by the lowliest crew members. Even the grip who had shoveled the horse manure would get to eat before she did.

"Hey, nice outfit."

At the sound of Mitch's voice, Frankie felt a sudden urge to grab the scooped neckline of her blouse and pull it up to her chin. She searched his face for some sign of lasciviousness, and when she didn't find any, wasn't quite sure whether to feel relieved or insulted.

"Thanks." She forced herself to relax the hands that had instinctively clenched. "Where have you been keeping yourself? I didn't see you on the set."

"I've been on the soundstage, rigging up the wiring." His grin was slow and somehow sinful. "Don't tell me you missed me!"

"Don't worry, I won't," retorted Frankie with a toss of her head. She would have walked away, but Mitch grabbed her arm.

"Hey, don't be sore. To tell you the truth, it's a relief to see a friendly face—or a familiar one, even if it's not very friendly," he amended hastily. "Have lunch with me? My treat."

Frankie could not have said whether it was the commissary full of strangers or her rapidly dwindling cash supply, but whatever the reason, she found herself taking a seat at the small table Mitch indicated. He disappeared into the mob crowding around the counter and returned minutes later with two cheese sandwiches and two small glass bottles of milk. Frankie supposed she shouldn't wonder at his being back so quickly; as best man, or whatever his new title was, he would take precedence over the mere extras.

"So, how's show biz?" asked Mitch around a mouthful of sandwich.

"It's okay."

"Just 'okay'? This from the girl who was going to be the next Tallulah Bankhead?"

"I'm learning a lot about the business." Frankie dabbed at the corner of her mouth with her napkin. "Like the fact that the scenes aren't filmed in order. Oh, and did you know we're shooting scenes with stunt doubles when some of the real stars haven't even been cast yet? But I don't know, somehow I thought it would be more—more—"

"Glamorous?" suggested Mitch.

"I never thought I would say this, but at times it's been almost boring." Frankie sighed. "Let's face it, I didn't come all the way from Georgia to run around in my bare feet and yell at the top of my lungs."

"Shoot, you could've done that at home," Mitch quipped.

"Ha!" Frankie gave a derisive laugh. "Not if my mother had anything to say about it. A lady should never raise her voice, and as for going barefooted, a lady might just as well be naked."

"Some folks might say you've got a pretty good start on that," Mitch observed, eyeing the hint of cleavage revealed by her peasant blouse.

"How dare you!" Frankie clutched her paper napkin to her chest in a manner that both conveyed her outraged dignity and protected her offended modesty.

"Hey, I'm sorry. I never should have said that." Mitch threw up both hands in mock surrender. "I guess I've spent too many years hanging around with the guys in the A & M locker room; after a while, you forget how to talk to a girl." Besides, the sort of girls he and his teammates sought out usually weren't that big on conversation.

Frankie gave a disdainful sniff and surveyed the crowded commissary, weighing the prospect of granting undeserved forgiveness against the even less appealing alternative of eating alone. Fortunately, she was spared the decision by a female voice calling her name in the refined tones of the British.

"Frances! Frankie, darling, never tell me you found work!"

"Kathleen!" As her roommate approached the table,

68

Frankie stood up to exchange air kisses, the preferred Hollywood greeting. "I'm working as an extra on *The Virgin Queen*. Meet England's newest tavern wench!" She spun in a circle, causing her long, full skirts to flare out.

"Newest *and* most beautiful. You look lovely. Doesn't she, Mitch? It is Mitch, isn't it?"

"Mitch thinks my costume is indecent," Frankie put in.

"I never said—"

"Shame on you, Mitch!" Kathleen scolded, wagging a finger at him. "As if the Hays Office would let her get away with that sort of thing, even if she wanted to! Ignore him, Frankie. He's afraid all the other men will notice you, and he wants a clear field."

This accusation, although teasing, was close enough to the truth that Mitch was thankful when Kathleen didn't press the point.

"Tell me, have you seen William Stanford? I heard he was playing Lord Leicester. Is he as dishy in person as he looks on the silver screen?"

"I only saw him once, and that was from far away," Frankie confessed. "He looked awfully handsome on horseback, though. They say he does all his own stunts, can you imagine?"

Mitch muttered something incomprehensible about pretty boy actors, and began to rise from his chair.

"Oh, don't leave on my account," Kathleen protested, grasping his sleeve. "I only stopped by in the hope of seeing Mr. Cohen—Arthur Cohen, that is, not his brother."

"He was watching the filming early this morning, but I haven't seen him in, oh, at least a couple of hours. Have you asked his secretary? Maybe he's in his office."

"I'd hoped to bump into him on the set, sort of accidentally on purpose." Kathleen flicked back the edge of her glove and glanced at her slim gold wristwatch. "I'd better fly now. Perhaps I'll beard the lion in his den after all. Goodbye, Mitch, it was nice seeing you again. Frankie, I'll see you this evening, and I'll expect to hear *all* about it!"

Frankie promised to give her a full accounting and wished her roommate luck on her meeting with Mr. Cohen. Having finished their meal, she and Mitch disposed of the remains and walked together to the large white cinderblock building that housed Soundstage B. Inside, a dozen actors in period costume milled about the edges of what appeared to be an Elizabethan tavern complete with rows of heavy wooden tables and a massive brick fireplace in one wall. Upon closer inspection, though, the tavern proved to be just as incongruous as the castle outside had been. A door set into the opposite wall appeared to lead to a narrow London street, but as Frankie walked past, she could see that the door opened onto nothing but bare concrete floor. The flickering light from the wall sconces was supplemented by huge round spotlights on all sides. The tavern had no ceiling at all; instead, the set was open all the way to the roof, where still more lights and several microphones on long cords dangled from the catwalks crisscrossing the building overhead.

"Guess I'd better get to work," Mitch said, indicating the catwalks with a jerk of his thumb. "Break a leg—or do they only say that to stage actors?"

"You're not going up *there*?" Frankie craned her neck.

"What's this?" Mitch gave her a knowing grin. "You're not afraid I'll fall, are you?"

Frankie tossed her head. "I'm just afraid you might land on William Stanford, that's all."

"Yeah, what a tragedy *that* would be—I might mess up his hair," retorted Mitch, heading for the ladder.

Once filming began, Frankie had very little time to worry about Mitch—or anyone else, for that matter. Her role in this scene was a little more demanding, but *only* a little: she was to swish her way between the rows of tables with a wooden tray perched on her hip, pausing from time to time to serve the queen's courtiers tankards of a foaming liquid that looked like beer but probably wasn't; alcoholic beverages were not used during filming as a result of one particular scene, legendary in

Hollywood lore, which required such extensive re-shooting that the entire cast was thoroughly soused by the time it was complete.

No such catastrophe occurred today, although one of the male extras, obviously a student of the dramatic school known as method acting, went so far in his portrayal of boisterous revelry as to pinch Frankie on her derriere. Frankie let out a little squeak of indignation, but as the cameras were still rolling, there was nothing she could do but be thankful that everyone else's attention was on Alice Howard, the young actress who played the queen's lady-in-waiting Gwyneth, who was at that moment stealing furtively into the tavern disguised as a boy. Not for the first time, Frankie wished she had a copy of the script so that she might follow the plot.

The director, however, was not satisfied. "Cut!" he bellowed. "Everyone back to your places. Rose, do— *something*—with Alice's costume!" He made a vague gesture in the direction of his chest.

The wardrobe mistress, correctly interpreting this command, hurried forward with a pin cushion. For the next five minutes, she tugged at Alice's doublet from all directions, anchoring the fabric in place so that it clung more closely to the young actress's curves. Frankie could only assume Queen Elizabeth's knights suffered from poor eyesight; surely there was no other explanation for how an entire roomful of men could fail to recognize a female dressed in a doublet that, while technically meeting the rigid standards of the Hays Code, certainly did nothing to hide her charms.

"Places, everyone . . . and . . . action!"

Choking back a giggle, Frankie made her way between the tables once more, this time avoiding the method actor. Once again, Gwyneth had scarcely made her entrance when a voice bellowed, "Cut!"

Everyone turned to the director, but he still sat in his folding canvas chair, his megaphone on the floor beside him.

"Whash—wha's going on here?"

Arthur Cohen staggered forward, his tie crooked, his face flushed. The soundstage was warm from the spotlights, but surely not so hot as to warrant the beads of perspiration that dotted the producer's forehead.

"Martinis for lunch, eh, Artie? Wish I'd been invited," the director, Mr. Harrison, quipped in a jovial voice that didn't quite ring true. "We're shooting the tavern scene this afternoon—you know, the one where Gwyneth delivers the queen's message to Leicester." He waved an arm in the direction of William Stanford and Alice Harper, who bobbed their heads in acknowledgement.

"You are, eh?" Arthur Cohen lurched forward onto the set,

belligerence in every wobbly step. "Well, I'll have you remember that *I'm* in charge here. I still run this studio, no matter what some may say to the contrary! Me, not Maury and his pie-in-the-sky Technicolor, and not these damned Brits who think they're the greatest thing in acting since William Shakespeare."

"Of course you're in charge, Artie, everyone knows this is your picture." The director rose from his chair and took a few steps in Mr. Cohen's direction. "Tell you what, why don't you go back to your office for a bit of a nap, and this evening we'll take a look at the rushes. I think you're going to be pleased."

But it was clear that Arthur Cohen was *not* pleased. His rant grew louder and more incoherent, ending with something about "two-bit whores who'll lie on their back for anyone who promises to make 'em a star!"

Alice burst into sobs, and William Stanford put a protective arm around her shoulders. "Here now, there's no call for that sort of talk—"

"You remember who signs your check!" Cohen wagged a pudgy finger in the actor's face. "*I'm* the one in charge here, not you, and not Maury, and not my wife! *I'm* the one who—I'm the one—I'm—"

His face turned an ugly shade of purple, and then Arthur Cohen fell forward, landing with a thud at Frankie's feet.

5

Murder, My Sweet (1944)
Directed by Edward Dmytryk
Starring Dick Powell, Claire Trevor,
and Anne Shirley

Alice screamed. William Stanford muttered something under his breath, the gist of which seemed to be that men who weren't capable of holding their liquor didn't have any business drinking at all. Frankie, white-faced with fear and shock, stepped gingerly aside, but not before catching a whiff of something earthy and green, something she had smelled once before, and that not long ago.

"Damn it, why can't he get drunk on his own time?" grumbled Mr. Harrison. "Bob, get a couple of grips to help you and see if you can get him back to his office. Maybe his secretary can pour a few quarts of black coffee into him."

The key grip called for three of his assistants, and together they grasped the producer by his arms and legs and lifted him from the floor. His head lolled back, unresisting.

"Wait a minute." The man who played William Cecil rose from one of the wooden benches, a veteran character actor instantly recognizable for any one of a dozen supporting roles, although not one person in fifty would have recalled his name. "I think we'd better call an ambulance."

"An ambulance?" echoed the director impatiently. "What the hell for? He's passed out drunk."

The actor didn't argue, but knelt down beside Arthur Cohen, looking in his costume for all the world like a vassal paying homage to his fallen liege, and felt his chest for a pulse. "I was at Ypres," he said with quiet dignity. "I know a dead man when I see one."

Harrison stepped onto the set and looked down into Arthur Cohen's dead face. The lifeless eyes still bulged, but the mottled purple that had suffused his cheeks only moments ago had begun to subside, leaving his face a pasty gray hue.

"What was it? A heart attack, or maybe a stroke brought on my too much alcohol?"

"The men in the white coats should be able to tell us—assuming that someone has sent for them," the veteran added pointedly.

The director, taking the hint, barked an order to his assistant, then raised his voice to address the entire cast and crew. "Looks like we'd better call it a day, folks."

Still, no one seemed inclined to leave. Actors, cameramen, and technicians all huddled together in small groups, speculating in lowered voices. Not until the ambulance had come to take the producer's body away did the crowd at last disperse.

"Places, everyone," called the director without much conviction. They all complied, from William Stanford down to the lowliest grip, but it was all for naught. After seven takes, in which Stanford accidentally kicked a hidden electrical wire unplugged, one of the knights knocked over a tankard of fake beer, and Alice forgot her lines twice, the director decided to call it a day.

"Better yet, take tomorrow off, too," he added. "I'll see you all on Thursday."

The cast and crew dispersed with grateful murmurs of relief. Mitch descended from one of the overhead catwalks and paused near the set, where Frankie still stood as if frozen. "Give you a lift?"

She smiled weakly. "Yes, please."

He waited outside Wardrobe while she changed back into her street clothes. Apparently the word of Arthur Cohen's death had spread rapidly; cars and pedestrians, actors and technicians alike seemed to slow down as they passed Soundstage B as if hoping for a glimpse of the body.

Soon Frankie returned, so pale and quiet that Mitch was moved to drape a comforting arm about her shoulders as they walked to his car.

"There was nothing anyone could have done," he said. "Poor devil probably never knew what hit him."

Frankie made no reply, but stood by silently as he opened the passenger door for her. He climbed in on the driver's side, and soon they were turning out of the studio gates and into the street. The sun was low in the west by this time, and the shadows of the palm and pepper trees along the road striped the pavement with purple and gold.

"Mitch," Frankie said abruptly, "what's a martini?"

"It's a cocktail," he answered, taken aback.

"I know that! I mean, how is it made? What's in it?"

"Gin and vermouth, with an olive on a toothpick." Mitch cocked one eyebrow. "Why? Are you thirsty?"

"No. And I don't think Mr. Cohen was, either."

Mitch stomped the brake, to the displeasure of the driver of the black DeSoto behind him. "What are you saying?"

"I don't think Mr. Cohen had been drinking before he died."

"You don't think—oh, come on, you saw the man! He was completely plastered!"

The driver of the DeSoto leaned on the horn. Mitch waved a "mea culpa" and floored the accelerator.

"If Mr. Cohen was so drunk," Frankie pressed on, "why didn't he have alcohol on his breath?"

Mitch gave a short, humorless laugh. "Honey, I'll bet you wouldn't know what liquor smelled like if—"

"I would, too!" Frankie retorted, bristling. "When I was fourteen, I stumbled across the bottle of Jack Daniels that Daddy kept hidden in the well."

Mitch guffawed, a real laugh this time. "You're kidding! Don't tell me you drank it!"

"Well, no. I was going to—just to see what it tasted like— but it smelled so nasty I couldn't bring myself to do it. In fact, if it tastes anything like it smells, I wonder why Daddy bothers? Unless he just likes the idea of putting one over on Mama."

"Wouldn't surprise me," said Mitch, who by this time had heard enough of Frankie's mother to have formed a reasonably accurate picture of that formidable female.

"But back to what I was saying," Frankie continued, determined not to be sidetracked. "Mr. Cohen didn't smell like that at all."

"Well, whiskey and vermouth are two different things,"

Mitch hedged.

"Yes, and I'll tell you something else I'll bet you don't know! Do you remember the night you took Pauline Moore to dinner?"

"How could I forget?" Mitch mused in so cryptic a tone that Frankie's single-mindedness was in imminent danger of wavering. The only thing that kept her on track was not the memory of Arthur Cohen's untimely end, but a perverse determination not to give Mitch the satisfaction of hearing her beg for details of his date with Pauline.

"Well," she continued, "that very same afternoon, Mr. Cohen quarreled with his brother Maurice."

Mitch arched a skeptical eyebrow. "He told you this in a job interview?"

"No, not exactly." Frankie glanced up at him guiltily. "You see, I didn't exactly have an interview with him. Oh, I tried, but there was no one at the reception desk. I heard voices down the hall, though, so I followed the sound to Mr. Cohen's office and waited outside the door. I was going to knock, but I didn't want to interrupt, so I just—I sort of—"

"Frances Foster!" exclaimed Mitch with unholy glee. "Do you mean to tell me that you eavesdropped outside the man's door? What would your mother say?"

Frankie sighed. "She would say that eavesdroppers never

hear anything good about themselves. And she'd be right. Only I didn't hear anything about myself—how could I, when neither one of the Cohen brothers had ever heard of me?—but I did hear them arguing, and I heard Mr. Cohen tell his brother that if he wanted him out of the business, he'd have to kill him first."

Mitch let out a long, low whistle, but didn't speak for a long moment. "Look honey," he said at last, "it must have been awkward for you, stuck there in the hall, and I'm sure you must have been nervous. Under the circumstances, it wouldn't be surprising if you misunderstood—"

"Don't patronize me, Mitchell Gannon! I know what I heard!"

"Okay, okay!" Mitch released the steering wheel and raised his hands in mock surrender. "But think about what you're saying. Do you honestly believe Arthur Cohen was murdered, and by his own brother, at that? That's a pretty strong accusation."

"I'm not accusing anyone—not exactly. I just think it's a bit too much of a coincidence, that's all."

"Are you going to call the police?"

"Are you kidding? I wouldn't dare. I've got no proof, so they'd probably laugh at me. But I'll bet Maurice Cohen wouldn't laugh! At best he'd fire me for eavesdropping, and at worst he'd fire me for eavesdropping and then sue me for slander. Either way, I'd find myself on the next train back to Georgia."

Mitch shook his head. "A fate too horrible to contemplate! So, what do you plan to do?"

"I've been thinking about that, and—" Frankie swiveled in her seat and gave him a long, measuring look. "Mitch, do you know how to pick locks?"

"What makes you think I would know such a thing?" demanded Mitch.

"Feminine intuition," she responded without hesitation. "Well, do you?"

"Maybe, maybe not. What kind of lock do you want picked?"

"A door lock. The door to Mr. Cohen's office, to be exact. Can you get it open?"

"I can," Mitch agreed cautiously, "but I'm still not convinced that I want to. Why do you need to get into his office?"

Frankie gave an impatient little huff. "Don't you see? If someone murdered Mr. Cohen—notice, I said 'if'!—then he must have been in Mr. Cohen's office not too much earlier."

"Yeah?" Mitch's tone suggested curiosity mixed with a healthy dose of skepticism.

"He had to have some time to administer the poison, or

whatever it was," Frankie pointed out impatiently.

"Oh, so now Cohen was poisoned! How do you figure that?"

"Well, he obviously wasn't shot, or stabbed, or conked on the head! Poison is the only other method I could think of off the top of my head."

"Brilliant deduction, Dr. Watson! And now I, Mr. Holmes, will use my superior intellect to reveal the murderer's identity."

"Oh, really?" Frankie's chilly tone could have frozen water.

"Miss Kathleen Stuart, by her own admission, had an appointment with Mr. Cohen. A short time later, he stumbles onto the soundstage and keels over dead. Clearly, Miss Foster, your roommate is a ruthless killer."

"Very funny! Now, if we could get some costumes from Wardrobe and pose as a cleaning crew, I think we could get into Mr. Cohen's office without attracting undue attention, and—"

" 'We'?" echoed Mitch. "I don't remember agreeing to any of this."

"Okay, fine! I don't need your help, anyway." Frankie's chin rose defiantly, but her eyes grew luminous and her lower lip quivered. "I'll do it myself, and if a ruthless murderer finds me there and kills me to keep his terrible secret from being discovered, you can tell my parents I want a simple headstone of white marble with the words 'She Was Right' carved beneath my name."

"Whoa, there! I never said I *wouldn't* do it; I just don't like being railroaded, that's all. A fellow likes to think he makes his own decisions."

"Then you will?" Frankie pleaded. "Please?"

Mitch made the mistake of looking into her doe-like brown eyes, and knew he was fighting a losing battle. "If I don't, you'll only make a mess of things and probably end up in the slammer, so I guess I'd better come along for the ride. Just tell me one thing."

"What do you want to know?"

"Why is this so important to you? After all, you hardly knew the man."

"You saw what the filming was like this afternoon, after—*it*—happened. If there's anything fishy about Mr. Cohen's death, it needs to be settled, so the studio can get back to normal as soon as possible. The show must go on, and all that, you know."

"It would go on just as smoothly if any monkey business was swept under the rug—maybe more so," Mitch pointed out. "I would have thought Mama's daughter would have been taught that a lady doesn't make waves."

"Yes, but Daddy is a judge, and Daddy's daughter believes that a murderer—if there is one—should not be allowed to go unpunished."

He regarded her with a curious half smile. "You're something else, Frances Foster, you know that?"

Coloring slightly, Frankie looked down and twisted her gloved hands in her lap. "Maybe you'd better call me Frankie. All my friends do, and so far you've been an awfully good friend."

Privately, Mitch thought he was a damn fool, and wondered if he would live to rue the day he'd hopped aboard a westbound train and met a sweet Southern girl with stars in her eyes.

6

Desk Set (1957)
Directed by Walter Lang
Starring Spencer Tracy and Katherine Hepburn

Mitch made an illegal but highly effective U-turn at the next light, and soon they were rolling up to the studio gates.

"Take off your gloves," Mitch commanded.

"What?"

"Don't ask questions, just do it. Take off your gloves and put 'em in the box." He nodded in the direction of the glove compartment built into the dashboard.

Frankie gave him a puzzled look but obeyed without protest as they drew even with the security guard's booth.

" 'Fraid I can't let you in, kids," the guard said. "We're shutting down for the day. There's been a death, you know. Old

Arthur himself."

"We know, we were there. Only Miss Foster here—" He indicated Frankie with a jerk of the thumb and an exasperated tone. "—forgot her gloves. Sheesh—*women!*"

Enlightenment dawned, and Frankie was quick to take her cue. "I was upset," she protested. "You would be, too, if Arthur Cohen had just fallen dead at your feet!"

"Okay, I guess I can let you in for a minute," the guard said reluctantly as the gate swung open. "Just don't be long."

"We won't. I know exactly where I left them," Frankie assured him with perfect truth.

A moment later, they were in, and only a few minutes after that, Frankie and Mitch were standing in a room that resembled a giant closet, working their way through row after row of clothes of every description. It didn't take long to locate a dingy coverall for Mitch, although this strained a bit through the shoulders when he tried it on for size. Frankie, however, was a different story, as the women's wardrobe boasted such an extensive selection. Mitch had high hopes for a leftover costume from *Parisian Follies of 1934* consisting of a form-fitting black dress with a very short full skirt and a frilly apron of white organza, but Frankie, seeing this, merely rolled her eyes and turned her attention back to the racks of clothes.

She finally settled on a frumpy yet functional gray dress

and chunky black shoes with low heels. Standing before the large mirror, she held it up to her chest and examined it for fit.

"I'd better check out the locks on those doors," Mitch said in a rare display of tact, and left the room, allowing her the opportunity to try on her borrowed plumes in privacy. She soon had the satisfaction of seeing that the dress did fit, if one overlooked a slight bagginess about the bodice. Not that it mattered; in an industry based on beauty, no one would look twice at such a dowdy creature. She quickly stripped off the dress and dressed again in her own clothes before Mitch returned.

Their mission completed, they climbed back into Mitch's borrowed car and left the studio for the second time in less than an hour. Frankie made a point of putting her gloves back on, and even waggled her fingers at the security guard as they passed through the gate.

"So far, so good," said Mitch, wheeling the Model A Ford into the street. "I'll pick you up at nine o'clock. What are you going to tell the girls back at the Studio Club?"

"As little as possible. Oh, I'll have to tell them Mr. Cohen is dead—that'll be all over town by morning! And I guess I'll have to give Kathleen some explanation of why I'm going out tonight dressed like someone's cleaning lady." Her brown eyes grew round as a new thought occurred to her. "Mitch, do you think Kathleen might have seen something? She was on her way to see Mr. Cohen only an hour or two before he died."

"You scoffed at the notion when I suggested it," he reminded her.

"I scoffed at the notion that Kathleen had anything to do with it," Frankie retorted. "But she might have seen someone suspicious lurking around his office, or noticed Mr. Cohen acting strangely, or—oh, anything."

Mitch shrugged as he drew up next to the curb in front of the Frankie's boarding house. "Couldn't hurt to ask. See you at nine, okay?"

Frankie agreed, although somewhat absentmindedly. She snatched up the frumpy dress and shoes and ran inside, eager to collar her roommate. When she opened the door to the lounge, however, she discovered the Studio Club's other residents had ideas of their own. She had hardly closed the door behind her before they demanded, "What happened? We heard all about it on the radio. Is Arthur Cohen really dead?"

Frankie sighed. "If you heard it on the radio, you probably know more than I do. It was awful! He came staggering in during filming and fell practically at my feet. The ambulance came and took him away, and nobody would tell us anything at all. What are they saying killed him?"

"Either a heart attack or a stroke," Roxie said. "They won't know for sure without an autopsy."

Arching one plucked eyebrow, Pauline regarded the gray dress draped over Frankie's arm. "Have you been shopping, Frances?" she purred. "I hope you got it on sale."

"I—I have a late audition," Frankie stammered, and headed for the stairs.

Kathleen entered their room only a few minutes behind her. "What sort of audition is it, Frances?" she asked in her soft British accent.

"Call me Frankie," she reminded her roommate. "As for the audition, I don't know all the details." Feeling that some sort of explanation was called for, she added, "I don't know if they'll finish *The Virgin Queen* or not, now that Mr. Cohen is dead. I figure I'd better start looking around for a new role."

Kathleen sat on the edge of the bed, and reached for Frankie's hand. "I don't know quite how to say this, but I'm not sure it's a good idea, going on an audition so late at night. You haven't been in Hollywood very long, so perhaps you're not aware that some 'auditions' are little more than an opportunity for an unscrupulous producer or director to get inside a girl's underpants."

Frankie blushed at such plain speaking. And she'd always heard the British were reticent! Still, Kathleen clearly expected an answer, and Frankie was very much afraid she might insist on accompanying her. Taking the gray dress by its shoulders, she shook it out, displaying it in all its frumpiness.

"I don't think anyone is very likely to have improper designs on me dressed in this," she said. "Besides, Mitch is coming with me. He's driving me to the studio."

Kathleen's brow cleared. "Oh, if he's going to be with you, then that's okay."

Frankie was a bit annoyed at the suggestion that Mitch's mere presence somehow made a girl instantly respectable, but she bit her tongue and sat down beside Kathleen on the bed as if settling in for a long session of girl talk. "So, wasn't it awful about Mr. Cohen? Did you ever get to see him?"

"No, there was someone else in his office."

"Kathleen!" Frankie's eyes widened. "Whoever was in Mr. Cohen's office at that time may have been the one who killed him!"

"Killed him?" Kathleen echoed in alarm. "I thought he died of a heart attack!"

"That's what they're saying," Frankie admitted grudgingly. "That, or a stroke. But I'm not so sure." She recounted the suspicions she'd voiced to Mitch: the quarrel between the two brothers, the strange odor, and the bizarre behavior Arthur Cohen had exhibited just before his collapse.

"Anyway, that's what this dress is really for," she

concluded. "Mitch and I are going back to the studio tonight to have a look around."

"What exactly are you looking for?"

"I don't know," Frankie confessed. "I only hope I'll know it when I see it."

"You will be careful, won't you?"

"I promise."

Having unburdened herself to her roommate, Frankie found it was a relief to have a confidante. When, shortly before nine o'clock, she began the transformation from starlet to cleaning lady, Kathleen was eager to assist, helping fasten the two rows of buttons that held the dress closed in the front and even locating a hair net for confining Frankie's too-stylish curls. And when nine o'clock came, Kathleen sat with Frankie in the now deserted lounge, listening for the sound of Mitch's car.

Frankie didn't invite him in, since the Studio Club had strict rules regarding male visitors, but opened the door as soon as he rang the bell.

"You look ravishing," he told her, grinning broadly.

"You're two minutes late," she scolded, trying not to notice the way his faded blue work shirt strained across his broad shoulders.

"Sorry about that. Finding a suitable ride took a bit longer than I'd intended." He led the way to a white van with

"Johnson's Janitorial Service" emblazoned on the side panel, and threw open the passenger door with a flourish. "My lady, your chariot awaits."

"Where did you get *that*?"

"Let's just say I borrowed it from a friend of a friend."

"I see," said Frankie, scrambling into the passenger seat. "And does this 'friend' know it's missing?"

"Ah, but it won't be missing by morning." Mitch slammed the door shut behind her and climbed behind the wheel. "If you're ready, we'll be on our way."

There was almost no traffic at this hour, and they reached the studio in record time. Mitch drew the van up beside the gate, where the night watchman sat dozing in his shack. When Mitch rapped on the window, the slumberer awoke in mid-snore and opened the gate with the too-eager air of one trying to conceal previous negligence.

"So far, so good," Mitch muttered once the gate had clanged shut behind them. He pressed his foot to the gas pedal, and soon braked to a stop at the front door of the Monumental Pictures offices.

"Shouldn't we park somewhere a little less conspicuous?" Frankie wondered aloud. "Maybe behind the building or at least in the shadow of the trees."

"We don't want to look suspicious." Mitch had already

jumped down from the van to remove a collection of mops and brooms from the back of the vehicle. "Here, do you want a broom or a mop?"

Frankie took a broom and followed Mitch to the front door, holding it across her chest like a weapon as he picked the lock.

He grinned at her. "You know, it would almost be worth it to get caught, just to see if you'd really use that thing."

"Just hurry, will you?"

"Whatever you say."

A moment later they were inside. Mitch clicked on the light in the foyer, and Frankie squinted against the sudden brightness.

"Do you really think that's wise?"

"We have to act like we have a legitimate reason to be here, remember? I don't think too many cleaning crews go about their business in the dark."

They made their way down the hall to Arthur Cohen's office. Frankie watched over his shoulder as Mitch worked his particular brand of magic on the door, and soon it swung open.

"Why do I get the feeling you didn't learn that in college?" Frankie asked with mingled disapproval and awe.

Mitch shrugged. "What can I say? I have a well-rounded education."

He flipped the light switch, and Arthur Cohen's private

office was revealed, sinister in its very normalcy. The two upholstered chairs where they'd sat during their interview still faced the big oak desk, which still looked as square and solid as it had on that day. A shiny black telephone sat at what would have been Mr. Cohen's right hand, and beside it lay a small leather-bound notebook. An appointment book, perhaps? Frankie reached for it, almost afraid to hope.

"Wait!" Mitch grabbed her wrist.

"What's the matter?"

"All good cleaning ladies wear rubber gloves to protect their hands." He dug into the pocket of his pants and produced a pair. "Besides, if the police do decide old Artie was murdered, you don't want your fingerprints all over his office."

Seeing the logic of this argument, Frankie made no protest, but tugged the gloves over her fingers. The pages of the little notebook were harder to turn with gloves on, but it didn't take much to tell her what she needed to know: the book was arranged as a daily calendar, with every page bearing a scrawled combination of names, times, or phone numbers. She flipped to May 12, and ran a finger down the page. It appeared that Mr. Cohen had had an eleven o'clock appointment with someone named Harold Fountain, and twelve o'clock was simply penciled in "M." Maurice? Frankie wondered.

"Get a move on," Mitch said impatiently. "We haven't got

all day."

Frankie closed the notebook and replaced it on the desk.

"Okay, let's get out of here." Mitch nudged her in the direction of the door.

"Wait." Frankie frowned, sniffing the air. "What's that smell?"

"What smell?"

She sniffed again. "It's the same thing I smelled earlier, when Mr. Cohen collapsed."

Mitch took a tentative sniff or two, then followed the source to a metal canister on a shelf behind Arthur Cohen's massive desk.

"Bingo!"

He pried open the close-fitting lid, and he and Frankie almost knocked heads in their eagerness to peer inside. The canister was slightly less than half full of what appeared to be dried and chopped leaves of a very pungent species.

"What is this?" Mitch asked, digging his hand inside and letting the stuff run through his fingers. "Pipe tobacco?"

"No." Frankie suddenly remembered the other time she'd smelled that particular odor. She had been standing in the hallway just outside this very office, and then, as now, the smell had made her want to sneeze. "*Achoo*! It's Mr. Cohen's— *achoo*!—herbal tea. He drank it for his indigestion, and—oh, gosh! Maurice said that some day he was going to kill himself drinking it!"

"That must have been some job interview you had!"

"I told you, it wasn't—*achoo*!—an interview—"

"Quiet!" Mitch raised one hand abruptly to silence her.

"Believe me, if I *could* stop sneezing, I—*achoo*!—*would*!"

"Shh! Someone's coming!" Mitch snapped the lid back on the canister and returned it to the shelf. On the desk blotter, a fine dusting of leaf and stem pieces left a circle of pristine white where the canister had sat.

"Oh, damn!" muttered Mitch.

"Language," scolded Frankie. She swiped her hand across the blotter, dusting off the herbal detritus as best she could.

A moment later the front door flew open and a voice, magnified by a bullhorn, announced, "Come out with your hands up! We have you surrounded!"

7

Angels with Dirty Faces (1938)
Directed by Michael Curtiz
Starring James Cagney, Pat O'Brien,
Humphrey Bogart, and Ann Sheridan

D on't shoot!" Squinting against the glaring white beams of two flashlights, Frankie eased herself through the open door and down the three broad, shallow stairs to the ground, hands held over her head as she groped her way down each step with the toe of her shoe. "We're unarmed."

As if to test the truth of this statement, a tight-lipped young police officer in a heavily starched blue uniform came forward to frisk her—a procedure that to Mitch, following in her wake, seemed to take an excessively long time.

"And now," said the policeman, administering a similar treatment to Mitch in a far more perfunctory manner, "suppose you tell me what the pair of you were up to, prowling around studio headquarters after hours."

The policeman's badge identified him as Officer Kincaid. Mitch, who had assumed the preponderance of Irish policemen on screen was an invention of Hollywood, put it down as one more instance of art imitating life. "Well, Officer, I guess you've heard about what happened to Arthur Cohen today. Say, can I lower my arms already? They're starting to go numb." Receiving permission, Mitch flexed his biceps a couple of times before letting his arms drop to his sides. "You see, we were there when it happened. In fact, Miss Foster here was standing so close that old Arthur nearly fell on her."

"Mm-hmm," muttered the police officer, scribbling something in a small notebook. "You two work for Johnson's Janitorial Services?"

Mitch looked puzzled. "No, why?"

The policeman jerked his head in the direction of the van parked nearby.

"Oh, that. I borrowed it from a friend."

"Is the 'friend' aware of that?"

Mitch bristled at the implied accusation. "I didn't steal it, if that's what you're getting at. You want his number? You can phone him and ask him yourself."

"That won't be necessary—at least, not yet."

"You're not going to arrest us, are you?" Frankie pleaded with wide brown eyes. "Daddy is up for re-election this fall, and the scandal could ruin his career."

"Your father is a politician?"

"No, he's a judge."

A fine sheen of perspiration broke out on Officer Kincaid's forehead. "A judge," he echoed in a flat voice.

"In the criminal court," Frankie added helpfully.

The young policeman merely nodded, his thoughts focused on how to extricate himself from a situation that might well prove fatal to his own career. Frankie, seeing his attention was otherwise engaged, saw no reason to burden him with the information that her father's jurisdiction was almost two thousand miles away.

"Look here," said Kincaid in conciliatory tones, "I'm sure you didn't mean any harm, Miss—?"

"Foster. Frances Foster."

"—Miss Foster, but you really shouldn't be here. I know you've had a terrible shock, so why don't I escort you home, and we'll forget the whole thing."

"Hey, wait a minute! I brought Miss Foster here, and I can take her home!" Mitch jabbed his thumb into his chest to emphasize the point.

Kincaid threw a cursory glance at Mitch, then took Frankie

tenderly by the arm. "No, I think you'd better return that vehicle to its rightful owner before it's reported as stolen. Watch your step, Miss Foster. I wouldn't want you to trip over the curb in the dark."

Frankie gave Mitch what she thought was a reassuring smile, but received only a glare in return. Miffed, she turned back to the young policeman and bestowed a dazzling smile upon him.

"Your boyfriend appears to be the jealous type," Kincaid said, opening the passenger door for her.

"My what? Oh, Mitch. He isn't my boyfriend. He's just someone I met on the train." Something, either an innate sense of honesty or a pang of conscience, compelled Frankie to add, "He's been awfully helpful to me since then, but he seems to have appointed himself my watchdog."

Mitch and his borrowed van were soon left behind as Kincaid steered the squad car through the gates and onto the road. "So, what gave the two of you the idea to go poking about the studio after closing?"

"It was my idea. I'd been to Monumental Pictures earlier to apply for a job, and I overheard an argument between Mr. Cohen and his brother. He said that Maurice would take over the studio over his dead body."

"And so you decided it must have been murder. Surely if

they knew you'd overheard a death threat, they wouldn't have offered you a job," pointed out the policeman, braking to a stop as the traffic light turned red.

"They didn't. At least, not then. They, er, didn't know I was standing in the hall at the time."

"Eavesdropping, eh?"

"Not on purpose!" Frankie protested hastily.

"Maybe not. Still, people say things alone with their family that they would never say in front of strangers. And in the case of Arthur and Maurice Cohen, it's well known in Hollywood circles that they fought like cats and dogs, except when one or the other of them was threatened. Then they circled the wagons."

"Threatened?" echoed Frankie, eyebrows raised.

The light turned green, and Officer Kincaid pressed his foot to the accelerator. "I'm not saying anyone threatened either one of them with bodily harm. But rival studios, bad reviews—" He shrugged. "It's a stressful life, or so I've heard. It's no wonder he had a stroke. The only real surprise is that he didn't have one before now."

"Are they sure it's a stroke?"

"They're sure enough. There's no way to know for sure without an autopsy."

"Will there be one?"

"Not unless the family requests it." Seeing Frankie's eyes light up, he hastened to add, "And why should they? They're satisfied that Arthur Cohen suffered a stroke."

Frankie had nothing to say to this, but she thought it very convenient that Maurice Cohen, who had the most to gain by his brother's death, was also in a position to see that the body was not examined too closely.

"What other family does he have?" she asked at last. "Besides Maurice, I mean."

"There's his wife—his widow, I should say—Letitia Lamont."

"*Letitia Lamont?*" Frankie exclaimed, the producer's death momentarily forgotten. "The silent film star?"

"That's the one. You've seen her work?"

"When I was a little girl, I saw her in *Knights of the Round Table*. She was so beautiful as Guinevere, and her scenes with Lancelot were so romantic." She giggled. "I was too young to understand that she was married to King Arthur. He was so much older, I thought he was her father."

They talked of inconsequential things for the rest of the drive, of films they had seen and actors they admired, and by the time Officer Kincaid walked Frankie to the door of the Hollywood Studio Club, he flattered himself that he had steered her mind into more acceptable channels. But Frankie was made of sterner stuff. While they debated the rival merits of Gary Cooper and Jimmy Stewart, Frankie's fertile brain was hard at work devising a plan. She could hardly wait until morning, when she would set the first phase of her plan in motion.

"Thank you for seeing me home," she told the young policeman. "It was awfully nice of you not to arrest Mitch and me."

"Not at all, Miss Foster. I'm sure it was an honest mistake, and you meant well." He shifted his weight from one foot to the other, clearly reluctant to leave. "I guess I'd better be getting back to the station. Can I see you again sometime?"

Naïve Frankie might be, but she could tell when a young man was interested in her. She weighed her options and decided it might be useful to have a friend on the police force. She noted his hesitation and wondered if he was angling for a goodnight kiss; she didn't think she was ready to be *that* friendly. She wasn't at all sure a policeman was allowed to kiss girls while he was on duty anyway. In the end, she settled for a warm smile and a handshake.

"That would be lovely. Thanks again, and goodnight."

Inside the Studio Club, the big common room was empty; most of the girls had gone out on dates, or to work the part-time jobs that supported them while they awaited their big break. Somewhere overhead, someone tap danced to a phonograph scratching out "I Got Rhythm." Frankie hurried upstairs to her room, where Kathleen sat curled up at the head of the bed perusing the classified ads.

"What's taken you so long?" Kathleen demanded, throwing the newspaper aside. "I was getting worried."

"We ran into a little trouble." Frankie kicked off her shoes and collapsed onto the bed. "The police showed up."

"The *police*?" Kathleen's voice rose in alarm. "Did they arrest you?"

"No, thank goodness. I can just see me having to wire Mama for bail money." She grimaced at the thought.

The British girl relaxed against the headboard. "I'm glad you're all right. I was beginning to wonder. Did you find out anything about Mr. Cohen?"

"We didn't have time to do much. Say, Kathleen, tomorrow I'm going on one of those bus tours where they show you where all the stars live. Would you like to go with me? My treat," she added hastily. Most of the girls at the Studio Club suffered a chronic shortage of money.

"I'd like to, but I've already made plans." She jerked her head in the direction of the newspaper, which Frankie could now see was marked at random with circles drawn in ballpoint pen. "Job hunting."

"Auditions?" Frankie asked eagerly, snatching up the paper.

"No such luck. Waitress work, mostly. Since I can't count on Arthur Cohen to give me a job, I guess I'll have to go out and find one myself."

Frankie laughed. "You make it sound like he died just to get out of giving you a job! But I know what you mean. If they decide to scrap *The Virgin Queen*, I may be job hunting right along with you."

The two girls lapsed into sympathetic silence. It was an occupational hazard of aspiring actresses, this necessity of finding work that paid a living wage while still leaving time free for attending auditions.

"Anyway, why this sudden urge to see how the other half lives?" Kathleen asked. "I thought it was only the tourists who went in for that sort of thing."

Frankie shook her head. "Nothing really, just—curious."

"You know what they say, 'curiosity killed the cat.' "

"Maybe."

But Frankie didn't think it was curiosity that had killed Arthur Cohen.

Mitch dropped by the Studio Club the following morning, just to make sure Frankie hadn't had any more difficulty with the police—with one policeman, anyway. He found her in the common room with half a dozen other girls, all seated in chairs drawn together in a tight circle around the radio.

"I just wanted to be sure you made it home okay," he explained with a shrug, digging his hands into the pockets of his plus-fours. "That cop didn't give you any trouble, did he?"

"No, not at all," Frankie assured him. "He was very nice, and so understanding."

"Is that so?" Mitch scowled, unimpressed by the policeman's forgiving nature. "Well, I'd like him to understand a thing or two—"

"Shhh!" A freckle-faced redhead raised a finger to her puckered lips. "We're trying to listen to *Pepper Young's Family!*"

"—Brought to you by Camay, the mild beauty soap for a smoother, softer complexion!" gushed the radio announcer.

Mitch glared at the redhead before turning back to Frankie. "Isn't there someplace around here where we can talk?"

Frankie jumped up from her chair and grabbed Mitch by the arm. "Sure, follow me."

He allowed her to lead him out of the crowded common room and into the foyer. "Okay, where to?"

Frankie shrugged. "I've been thinking of taking one of those bus tours—you know, the ones that show you where all the stars live. Want to go with me?"

"I don't know," Mitch said with a grimace. "Sounds

awfully touristy to me. Do you honestly think you're going to catch a glimpse of Rudy Valentino mowing his lawn?"

"Valentino's been dead for ten years," Frankie said, rolling her eyes. "And I doubt he did his own yard work even when he was alive."

"Tell you what, why don't we check out Schwab's Pharmacy instead? You can see all the stars you want for free. Better yet, you can see 'em while sitting on a stool sipping an ice cream soda. Show me the bus tour that can beat that!"

"Please?" Frankie coaxed, looking up at him with wide doe's eyes. "My treat."

Mitch was a bit baffled by her sudden change from shamus to sightseer, but then, he only appreciated women; he never claimed to understand them. "Oh, okay, if it means that much to you. But I'm paying, understand? I don't sponge off dames."

Hollywood had been a tourist destination since the days of the earliest silent flicks, and Tanner Motor Company's double-decker tour buses had crisscrossed Beverly Hills since 1920, allowing movie lovers the chance to get a glimpse of their idols in their natural habitats. Frankie and Mitch boarded the bus at the Ambassador Hotel and Mitch paid the uniformed driver, grumbling a bit at the two-dollar fare. Squeezing her way down the aisle past rows of gawking sightseers, Frankie finally found a window seat about halfway to the back, leaving Mitch to sit next to the aisle. For the next half-hour, there was no sound but the tour guide's memorized spiel and the grinding of the bus's gears as it climbed higher into the Hollywood Hills.

The tour's crown jewel, Pickfair, was a disappointment, to say the least. The mansion built on Summit Drive by Douglas Fairbanks in 1919 for his bride, Mary Pickford, had begun the exodus of stars from Los Angeles to Beverly Hills. Unfortunately, nothing could be seen of it from the road but a wall and a gate embellished with an elaborately scrolled "P."

"Waste of two bucks," grumbled Mitch, an observation that earned him a sharp "*shhh!*" not only from his companion, but also his fellow passengers in the seats fore and aft. Lapsing into chastened silence, he amused himself by watching Frankie, who sat with her nose pressed eagerly to the glass as the tour guide identified points of interest.

Valentino, Richard Berthelmess, the recently departed and deeply mourned Will Rogers—they were all represented here, as were the very much alive Gloria Swanson, cowboy Tom Mix, and silent-screen vixen Pola Negri, whose career had foundered when the coming of the talkies had revealed her pronounced Polish accent. Then the bus slowed before a stark, boxy residence built in the cubist style.

"It's not a regular part of our tour," the guide confessed, "but if you'll look out the window to your right, you'll see the home of Hollywood producer Arthur Cohen, who died just yesterday of a heart attack."

Mitch looked sharply at Frankie, who met his accusing gaze with one of wide-eyed innocence.

At last the tour guide's rambling monologue wound to a close, and the bus lurched to a stop and disgorged its passengers onto the curb in front of the Ambassador.

"Wasn't that wonderful," a middle-aged woman gushed to her female companion, her handbag knocking several of her fellow passengers in the head as she made her way up the aisle toward the door. "I loved Valentino's Falcon's Lair, didn't you?"

"Oh yes," the other enthused with a reminiscent sigh. "I remember seeing him in *The Sheik* when I was a girl. They knew how to make pictures in those days."

Mitch stepped into the aisle in their wake, effectively blocking the aisle so Frankie could exit the bus. Once on the street, he allowed the other tourists to clear out before speaking his mind.

"Wasn't that interesting?" Frankie asked brightly. "Although I had hoped for a better view of Pickfair—"

" 'Fess up, Frances," Mitch interrupted, seizing her by the elbow and frog-marching her in the direction of his car. "You don't give two hoots for Pickfair. You wanted to see where

Arthur Cohen lived, and you knew it would be included on the tour."

"I didn't *know*," Frankie protested. "I saw in this morning's paper that he lived in Beverly Hills—that's what it said, 'producer Arthur Cohen of Beverly Hills'—and I thought the tour guide might point it out."

"And why do you need to know where old Artie lived?"

Frankie shrugged, a careless gesture that didn't fool Mitch for a minute. "I thought I might pay a condolence call to see how his wife is holding up. He was married to Letitia Lamont, the silent film star, you know."

"No, I didn't know, and what's more, I don't care! And I don't think you do, either. Well, you know what? Whatever you're up to, you can count me out. Last night you came this close to getting us both arrested for breaking and entering. If I'd wanted a criminal record, I could've gotten one back in College Station—and had a heck of a lot more fun doing it," he added, recalling certain off-campus establishments that catered to the more illicit activities of A & M students.

"There's nothing illegal about making condolence calls," Frankie insisted, sliding onto the passenger seat while Mitch held the door open. "In fact, I'm sure Mama would say it was the right thing to do. And she would say I ought to bring something—a pound cake, maybe."

"Speaking of your mama, did she ever spank you really hard when you were a child?"

"No, Daddy did that." Frankie winced at the memory. "If I was really bad, he used a belt. Why do you ask?"

"Because," Mitch said, slamming the car door for emphasis, "someday I'd like to shake his hand."

8

The Merry Widow (1934)
Directed by Ernst Lubitsch
Starring Jeanette MacDonald, Maurice Chevalier,
and Edward Everett Horton

re you sure you don't want to come along?" Sitting on the edge of the bed, Frankie tweaked one stocking in an effort to straighten the seam running down the back of her leg. "I'd be glad of your company."

Kathleen shook her head, setting her blonde curls bouncing. "I wish I could—I'd love to see how the other half lives!—but I've got a job interview at half past three."

Frankie looked up at her roommate, her interest piqued. "A screen test?"

"Nothing so glamorous. The Trocadero Club is looking for cigarette girls." She sighed wistfully. "I've been in Hollywood for over two years now. I thought by this time I'd be a household name and have a villa at the Garden of Allah."

"Maybe you'll be discovered at the Trocadero," suggested Frankie, eternally optimistic. "All the really important people go there."

"Maybe. In the meantime, I'd settle for having next month's rent taken care of."

Frankie lingered by the open door, suddenly reluctant to leave. It was one thing to announce to Mitch her intention of gate-crashing the Cohens' Beverly Hills residence; actually doing the deed was another thing entirely.

"Well, good luck," she said, hoping to the last that Kathleen would change her mind. "Let me know how it goes."

"You'll be the first to know," Kathleen promised. "Do you happen to know if Pauline is finished in the bathroom yet? I can't do a thing with my hair."

Frankie returned a noncommittal answer and, steeling herself to the prospect of descending upon Letitia Lamont all alone, started down the stairs to summon a taxi. As she crossed the lounge, the black telephone mounted on the wall seemed to draw her like a magnet. True, she and Mitch hadn't exactly parted on the best of terms, but that was nothing new; they'd been quarreling off and on since the moment they met. Surely if she asked him, he would go with her. She could save a cab fare, too, since he had a car. Her hand closed around the receiver. All she had to do was call him up, swallow her pride, and—

Frankie dropped the receiver as if it burned her hand. She wouldn't call Mitch Gannon if he was the last man on earth.

"What's the matter?" asked a feminine voice, amused. "Fight with the boyfriend?"

Frankie turned and saw Pauline elegant yet casual in satin lounging pajamas, descending the stairs with feline grace.

"He's not my boyfriend," Frankie insisted. "I was just— just calling for a taxi."

To prove the point, she snatched up the receiver and put the call through before she lost her nerve entirely. Pauline merely gave her a knowing smile and joined the group of girls listening to *Backstage Wife* in the lounge.

Her call completed, Frankie stepped outside to wait for her ride. Unfortunately, she had to make the trip empty-handed: the Studio Club might provide its female residents with practice rooms, a library, a ping-pong room, and even a rooftop deck for sunning (to the detriment of several small planes whose pilots were distracted by the view) but the one kitchenette provided for their use was unavailable. Two script girls and an aspiring screenwriter had taken possession of it in order to bake cookies for their boyfriends, an operation that showed every sign of taking the rest of the day. Frankie was a bit surprised at the

kitchen's popularity; she had assumed most of the girls living at
the Studio Club had come to California in the hopes of escaping
such domestic pursuits as baking.

A familiar Model A Ford turned the corner, and Frankie's
outlook brightened immediately. Mitch had come after all! She
hurried out to the curb just in time to see it go by and to hear the
wolf whistle directed her way by the stranger behind the wheel.

I don't need Mitch Gannon, she reminded herself sternly. *I
don't need anybody!*

Scarcely five minutes later, a taxicab pulled up beside the
curb.

"Where to, lady?" asked the driver.

"Summit Drive, Beverly Hills," Frankie answered,
climbing into the back seat. "I don't remember the number, but
I'll recognize the house when I see it."

Or so she thought. But forty-five minutes later, she hadn't
seen anything resembling the boxy Art Deco structure that
Arthur Cohen called home. Nor, for that matter, had she seen
the gates of Pickfair, or Tom Mix's house, or Valentino's
Falcon's Lair, or Gloria Swanson's mansion. In the meantime,
the meter mounted on the dashboard had continued to run.

Frankie leaned forward to speak to the cab driver. "Are you
sure we're on Summit Drive?"

"Did you say Summit?" asked the cabbie, all innocence. "I

thought you said Sunset."

He whipped a U-turn that all but flung her across the seat. Ten minutes later, the cab turned in the driveway in front of the Cohen residence and lurched to a stop. Frankie glanced at the meter and was dismayed to find the fare was almost three dollars—most of it run up on a wild goose chase up and down Sunset Boulevard.

"I guess you'd better wait." As reluctant as she was to give the dishonest driver any more of her hard-earned money, Frankie was even less eager to be left alone here in case things went sour.

Quickly, before she lost her nerve, she opened the door of the taxi and stepped out onto the paved driveway. The heels of her patent leather pumps clicked out a rhythm on the asphalt as she marched up to the front stoop and rang the doorbell. She heard the indistinct sound of voices from inside, although she could not make out the words they spoke. A moment later the door opened to reveal a solemn-faced young Mexican woman wearing a starched white apron over her plain black dress.

"Good afternoon." Frankie hurried into speech. "I'd like to see Miss Lamont—Mrs. Cohen, that is—if I may."

"Who is calling, please?" the maid asked in accented English. The wary expression in her dark eyes gave Frankie to understand she was not the first visitor to call on Letitia Lamont that day.

"I'm Frances Foster." Realizing her name would mean nothing to Arthur Cohen's widow, she added, "I don't know Miss Lamont personally, but I was working on one of her husband's films when he died. I would like to offer her my condolences."

"I will ask. Wait here, *por favor.*"

Left alone in the spacious foyer, Frankie surveyed the well-lit expanse of white paint, black lacquer, and chrome. Framed photographs of Letitia Lamont in several of her greatest film roles carried out the black-and-white color scheme, even while her historical costumes provided a counterpoint to the modern furnishings. Here she was dressed as Eleanor of Aquitaine in veil and wimple, here as Ophelia, clad in white and surrounded by wildflowers.

It was a room unlike any Frankie had ever seen. Why, then, was she suddenly thinking of her grandmother's house? It had been almost five years since her family had closed up the white-columned Greek revival building where her mother had grown up, but Frankie remembered it well enough to know that it would be hard to imagine anything more different from this masterpiece of modern design. Before she had time to ponder the question, the Mexican maid reappeared.

"*Señora* Lamont will see you. This way, please."

Frankie followed her down a hallway to a room at the back of the house whose large plate glass windows gave a panoramic view of the Hollywood Hills beyond.

It was not the room or the view, but its sole occupant who commanded Frankie's attention. Letitia Lamont's simple gray frock, while obviously expensive, was utterly devoid of ornamentation, and the long flowing curls she'd once been famous for were now bobbed into a more modern style. Her makeup—straight from the hand of Mr. Max Factor himself, Frankie didn't doubt, and much more subtle than the pancake look that had graced the screen a decade ago—could not quite disguise the lines of strain about her eyes and mouth, and in the harsh sunlight streaming in from the windows she looked much nearer forty than thirty. Still, she moved with a grace that caught the eye and wouldn't let go.

"Miss Lamont—Mrs. Cohen—" stammered Frankie, conscious of a sudden urge to kneel in the presence of this queen of the silent screen. "Thank you for seeing me. I saw your performance as Guinevere years ago. It made me want to become an actress myself."

Letitia Lamont removed the long cigarette holder from her scarlet mouth.

"Well, aren't you sweet?" Frankie had imagined Letitia Lamont would have a low, husky voice, but to her surprise, the star spoke with a pronounced Brooklyn accent. "Sorry to keep you cooling your heels in the foyer. Do sit down! It's been a rough day, to put it mildly."

"I can imagine," Frankie said, sinking onto a free-form black sofa. "I only wanted to tell you how sorry I am about—about Mr. Cohen. I was there when he—when it happened."

"The cops said he collapsed on the soundstage. Is that true?"

"I'm afraid so. We had just resumed filming after lunch when Mr. Cohen came in. He seemed—perturbed." It was a gross understatement, but she had to start somewhere.

Miss Lamont nodded. "He could be a pill when things didn't go to suit him, and *The Virgin Queen* was a pet project of his. It's a shame he couldn't have lived long enough to see it through to the end."

"I heard somewhere that his brother had wanted to film it in Technicolor." There was no point in mentioning that she'd heard it while eavesdropping outside Mr. Cohen's office.

The great actress smiled sadly, revealing a trace of the stunning beauty she had once been. "You heard right. In fact, it was the subject of more than one disagreement between them. Poor Arthur! He just couldn't understand that the industry is changing, and he had to change along with it. He even thought I should attempt a comeback. Can you imagine that? Me, in a talkie, with this voice? No, I knew my time was up. Sometimes the best thing you can do is to bow out gracefully." Her smile faded. "Maybe it's better for Arthur's sake that he didn't live long enough to know he was becoming about as relevant as the horse and carriage."

"How did his brother react to his death? If you don't mind my asking," Frankie added hastily.

"He was devastated. They were very close, never mind that they sometimes got along like oil and vinegar. In some ways they balanced each other. Maurice dragged Arthur kicking and screaming into the modern age, and Arthur reined in some of Maurice's wilder flights of fancy."

"Does he plan to continue filming *The Virgin Queen*?"

Miss Lamont shrugged and tapped a scarlet fingernail against her long holder to dislodge the ash clinging to the end of her cigarette. "I haven't the foggiest idea. He's still struggling to grasp the fact that Arthur is dead. I doubt poor Maurice can even think clearly enough to imagine how he'll carry on without him."

Frankie had to admit it didn't sound like the picture of a man who had killed his brother in order to grab control of the studio. And yet, could Maurice Cohen's reaction be attributed, not to grief, but to a guilty conscience?

"I'm sure many of us will miss him," Frankie said, not

quite sure how to steer the conversation in a more informative direction. "I know I will. After all, he gave me my first big break."

"I see." The great actress's mouth tightened and the temperature in the sunny room seemed to drop several degrees. "Miss Foster, if you came here expecting me to make good on my husband's promises, I'm afraid you're barking up the wrong tree. I can only suggest you give Hank Winston a call. It's what my husband would have told you, anyway."

"Mr. Cohen never promised me anything," Frankie protested, bewildered by the widow's suddenly cool demeanor. "In fact, I think he only offered me a job because he was interested in my friend."

One carefully sculpted eyebrow lifted. "Oh? And what friend was this?"

"Just someone I met on the train west. His name is Mitch Gannon. Your husband offered him a position as best boy because he took some classes in electrical engineering in college."

Miss Lamont's brow cleared, and the lines about her mouth relaxed. "Oh, now I understand," she said. "Yes, I can hear him now: 'Actresses in this town are a dime a dozen, but a man with a working knowledge of electricity is worth his weight in gold.' "

Frankie smiled. "Something like that."

"I apologize for jumping to the wrong conclusion, but when some girls say they'll do anything to make it on the silver screen, they do mean *anything*. And I'm well aware that my husband was no saint. I don't doubt he was happy to oblige a few of them."

Frankie could feel the heat rise to her face and knew she was blushing. True, the girls at the Studio Club had talked about this very thing, but it was jarring to hear it discussed so casually by the producer's wronged wife.

"You must have loved him very much, to be willing to forgive such—indiscretions," Frankie observed.

The great actress cocked her head to one side, as if considering the question. "Loved him? No, I don't think so. Few people in Hollywood marry for love, and those that do don't last very long. We made a good team, though, Arthur and I, and I will miss him very much."

"Had he shown any signs of heart trouble? Or do you believe it was a stroke?"

"No, no signs of ill health at all. Oh, he was under a lot of stress—it's a stressful business, you know—and I don't doubt he drank more than he should have. But as for what killed him, I really don't know. I suppose it could have been either one."

"Have you thought of asking for an autopsy?" Frankie

pressed on. "That way you would know for sure."

"My husband was Jewish, and Jewish law forbids autopsies as being disrespectful to the body." Miss Lamont blew a series of smoke rings. "And from my own gentile viewpoint, I can't see that it would make any difference. Arthur is gone, and no amount of poking and prodding about his body will bring him back."

"But wouldn't you like to know for sure if there was anything—unusual—about his death?"

The actress gave a humorless laugh. "Really, Miss—Foster, was it?—you sound almost as if you think my husband was murdered. Isn't that what autopsies are usually for? Any man in a position of power is sure to make enemies as well as friends, but the idea that anyone would murder him is ridiculous! All we need is for Hedda Hopper or Louella Parsons to get *that* idea into their heads! Now I think you had better go. I would like to lie down and rest a bit before going to the funeral parlor to finalize the arrangements."

"Of course," Frankie mumbled, painfully aware of having worn out her welcome. She muttered a last, semi-coherent expression of sympathy, then backed out of the room and into the hallway.

The Mexican maid was nowhere in sight, so Frankie showed herself through the foyer to the door. As she crossed the austere expanse of black, white, and chrome, she suddenly realized why it reminded her of her grandmother's house. In between the framed photographs of Letitia Lamont's glory days on the silver screen, she could see faint rectangles of similar size where the white paint was just a shade brighter than the rest of the wall. Clearly, other photographs had once hung here.

In the case of her grandmother's house, the pictures on the walls had hung there so long that the wallpaper beneath was a completely different color. Those pictures, some darkened with age, had been sold at an estate sale. Why had Miss Lamont's missing photographs been removed? What had happened to them?

9

The Big Sleep (1946)
Directed by Howard Hawks
Starring Humphrey Bogart and Lauren Bacall

Passing through the gates of Glendale's Forest Lawn Memorial Park, the taxi nosed its way past Cadillacs, Dusenbergs, Lincolns, and even an open-topped Cord whose sleek lines and sporty style struck a jarring note in its current somber surroundings. Beyond the parked automobiles, uniformed policemen stood guard at intervals along a length of velvet rope positioned to hold back a crowd more interested in catching a glimpse of a favorite star than in paying their final respects to Arthur Cohen. A discreet distance away, a gaggle of workers from the Shady Rest Funeral Home leaned on their shovels; after the crowds had gone home, they would go about the grim business of lowering the casket into the ground and covering it with dirt.

"Looks like you'll have to hoof it from here, ladies," the taxi driver said, lurching to a stop behind a gray Rolls-Royce. "I can't get you any closer."

"Anyway, thanks for trying." Frankie dug in her little black handbag for the forty-cent fare.

While Frankie paid the driver, Kathleen surveyed the mob that stood between them and Arthur Cohen's final resting place. "I'm not sure this was such a good idea," she said, displaying the quintessentially British talent for understatement.

"Of course it is!" Frankie declared with more bravado than she felt. "After all, we were acquainted with the deceased, at least a little bit, which is more than any of those people can say. They have to let us in."

Quickly, before Kathleen could suffer a change of heart and order the taxi to turn around, Frankie wrenched open the door and stepped out onto the bright green grass. The heels of her black patent leather pumps instantly mired in the soft ground; a lawn this lush was impossible to achieve in California without daily watering. Stepping gingerly to avoid sinking to her ankles, she made her way past the luxurious automobiles and scanned the crowd for the most likely point of attack.

"What a pity we're not famous," sighed Kathleen, hurrying to catch up. "Then the crowd would part magically before us."

"If you were really famous, they'd be more likely to rip that pretty black frock right off your back," Frankie observed pragmatically. "Wait a minute! If that's who I think it is, we're in!"

Picking up her pace, she headed straight toward a young policeman struggling to hold back a gaggle of girls dead set on catching a glimpse of Clark Gable among the mourners.

"Why Officer Kincaid, fancy meeting you here!"

" 'Afternoon, Miss Foster." The young policeman nodded at her, then glanced at her companion with combined curiosity and admiration.

"I'd like you to meet my roommate, Kathleen Stuart." Frankie gestured toward the British girl. "Kathleen, this is Officer Kincaid, one of L.A.'s finest." As the two shook hands, Frankie came to the point. "Officer, can you get us past the rope?"

He raised a skeptical eyebrow. "You're not still trying to play detective, are you?"

"No, no," Frankie assured him with less than perfect truth. "Kathleen and I both worked for Mr. Cohen in some small capacity, and we'd like to pay our last respects—which is more than you can say for most of the people here," she added, glancing across the expanse of green to where the Marx brothers wept sentimental tears for the benefit of a *Variety* photographer.

A scant ten yards away, gossip columnist Louella Parsons scribbled furiously in her notebook as a script girl from *The Virgin Queen* described a lurid scene that bore very little resemblance to reality.

"—Blood simply *everywhere*, and poor Mr. Cohen *moaning* in agony—"

The policeman, who had been inclined to turn the two girls away, struggled in defeat. "I guess it's okay," he said, dropping the velvet rope for them to pass. "I'll be going off-duty after the funeral. Can I give you a ride home?"

"That would be lovely," said Frankie, thinking of the forty cents she would save.

A light breeze ruffled the skirt of her black-and-white spotted crepe dress as she and Kathleen made their way closer to the grave site. Frankie had never been to a Jewish funeral before—Mama didn't quite approve of Jews, even if they were God's chosen people—and she was struck by how similar and yet how different it was from her grandmother's funeral five years ago. The chief mourners, family members of the deceased, were gathered in a tight cluster about the grave. Letitia Lamont was there, dressed in black from head to toe—at least, Frankie assumed it was the producer's widow beneath a wide-brimmed hat swathed in black netting. Maurice Cohen stood at her elbow, pale and heavy-eyed. Yet the casket itself was nowhere in sight, and the mourners looked down on a gaping hole; apparently the casket had already been lowered into the grave.

"Who can say unto the Lord, 'What workest thou?' " intoned the rabbi, bringing Frankie's attention back to the burial service. "He ruleth below and above; He ordereth death and restoreth to life."

Frankie was almost certain it had not been the Lord but someone else entirely who had ordered Arthur Cohen's death. Maybe it was a pity the actual death hadn't been a bit more dramatic, like the script girl's description; if there had really been blood everywhere, the police might have been a bit more thorough in their investigation.

When the rabbi had finished, Maurice Cohen shoveled the first scoops of dirt onto his brother's casket. There was something very final about the *thud* of earth on the lid of the casket, as if any secrets Arthur Cohen's body might have revealed were being buried with him.

Frankie frowned as a new thought occurred to her. It was true that there wasn't any blood, but what if there was some other form of evidence? When he burst onto the soundstage, Arthur Cohen was practically foaming at the mouth. Surely it wasn't too much of a stretch to think he might have spilled or coughed something onto his clothes—certainly not blood, but something else, something that could be tested for poison. Since

Mr. Cohen had fallen forward and landed face down on the floor, she hadn't seen anything. She glanced at the hearse from the Shady Rest Mortuary. No, she hadn't seen anything, but she knew who would have, if there had been anything to see.

The rabbi bowed his head and began to back away from the grave. "In the world which He will create anew, where He will revive the dead, construct His temple, deliver life, and rebuild the city of Jerusalem, and uproot foreign idol worship from His land, and restore the holy service of Heaven to its place, along with His radiance and splendor, and may He bring forth His redemption and hasten the coming of His anointed one . . ."

A murmured chorus of "amens" marked the end of the prayer, and the knot of mourners clustered about the casket began to disperse.

"Do we go, or stay?" asked Kathleen, shifting her weight from one foot to the other. "We're more than sightseers, but not exactly mourners, either."

"We stay," Frankie said decisively. "Remember, Officer Kincaid is giving us a ride, and he can't leave until the mob goes home."

Kathleen muttered something about getting back in time for *Fibber McGee and Molly.*

"Give you girls a lift?"

Frankie hadn't heard Mitch's approach—hadn't even

known he'd come to the funeral at all, in fact—and was annoyed to find her heart racing like a roadster competing for the Vanderbilt Cup. Even more distressing was the fact that Mitch didn't seem to be suffering any similar ill effects, standing there in his dark suit and tie with his hands dug into his pants pockets smiling at her as if they had parted on the chummiest of good terms.

"What are *you* doing here?" she asked frostily.

"Same thing you are, I imagine. Paying my last respects to the guy who gave me my big break. So do you want a ride back to the Studio Club, or not?"

"Not." Frankie tossed her head and set out in the direction the young policeman was stationed. "Officer Kincaid is giving me a lift as soon as he gets off duty."

Mitch grinned and fell into step beside her. "If you really want to ride in a paddy wagon, I can arrange it."

"I'd rather ride in the *front*, if it's all the same to you!"

"I'd love a ride, Mitch, if you're sure you don't mind," Kathleen put in eagerly.

"I thought you were coming with me and Officer Kincaid," Frankie protested, feeling somehow betrayed.

Kathleen shook her head. "Two's company, three's a crowd."

"Great!" Mitch pulled a handkerchief from the breast

pocket of his suit coat and swiped it across his forehead. "It's gotten awfully warm. We could stop at Schwab's for an ice cream soda, if you'd like."

"Chocolate, with whipped cream and a cherry on top?" Kathleen asked eagerly, Fibber McGee apparently forgotten. "Heavenly! What girl could resist?"

Mitch reached out a hand to steer Kathleen around a low headstone. "I don't know, you might be surprised at the girls these days who'd rather drag a fellow all over town. Come on, Kathleen, my car's over here. See you around, Frances."

He led the British girl away, leaving Frankie alone to cool her heels while she waited for her ride.

"Sorry to take so long," the young policeman said, joining her at last. "Some of these folks don't give up easily. Can you imagine, begging for autographs at a funeral? Sheesh!"

Lost in a waking nightmare in which Mitch and Kathleen sat hip to hip at Schwab's soda fountain, heads bent together as they sipped a single ice cream soda through two straws, Frankie greeted Kincaid more warmly than the situation warranted.

"Thanks awfully for giving me a ride, Officer," she said, smiling up at him as she slipped her hand through the crook of his arm.

"I'm off-duty now," he reminded her. "Why don't you call me Russ?"

"Russ, then," she echoed, trying it out. "Would you mind making one tiny stop on the way back? I have an errand to run."

"I'd be glad to take you anywhere you want to go." He grinned dopily into the wide brown eyes sparkling up at him. "Just name it."

Her forehead puckered in concentration as she recalled the writing on the side of the long black car. "Four twenty-two Camden."

A short time later, the squad car drew up to the curb in front of the Shady Rest Mortuary.

"A *funeral parlor*?" Russ's eyebrows lowered ominously. "Miss Foster, I warned you—"

"I'll only be a minute," Frankie said brightly, hopping out of the car and slamming the door on his protests.

Frankie had never been in a funeral parlor, her grandmother's body having been laid out in the parlor of the old antebellum home where she'd lived for more than fifty years. Inside, the Shady Rest was sparsely yet carefully furnished to convey an air of churchlike dignity without declaring in favor of any particular religion. The heels of her black patent leather shoes clicked on the polished hardwood floors, sounding unnaturally loud in the stillness.

"Hello?" she called. "Is anyone there?"

A stirring sound emanated from the back room, and a

moment later a tall, thin man bustled forward, rubbing his hands together in anticipation. "Good afternoon, young lady." Frankie found his ingratiating smile somehow at odds with the solemnity of his dark suit and necktie. "How may I help you in your time of bereavement?"

"You can't. That is, I'm not bereaved." Frankie took a deep breath and started afresh. "I'm here on behalf of the Arthur Cohen family." That much was true, so far as it went, although Arthur Cohen's family would have been surprised to hear it.

"Dear me!" exclaimed the mortician in some chagrin. "Were they unhappy with the arrange-ments?"

"No, no, the service was lovely," Frankie assured him hastily. "I've just come for Mr. Cohen's clothes—you know, the things he was wearing when he died." She only hoped his clothes hadn't been returned to his wife or, worse, destroyed.

"How very odd." He rubbed his hands together in a nervous gesture. "Miss Lamont—Mrs. Cohen, that is— indicated that there was no need to return the late Mr. Cohen's clothing."

"Maybe she changed her mind," Frankie suggested, crossing black-gloved fingers behind her back. "She was probably too distraught to know what she wanted, poor thing."

Even as she said the words, Frankie knew this was laying it on a bit thick. When she'd spoken to Miss Lamont, the "poor thing" had been as cool as the proverbial cucumber.

"I suppose you're right. As luck would have it, I haven't yet disposed of the deceased's clothing. If you'll wait right here, I'll fetch it."

He disappeared through the back door, and returned a few minutes later carrying a bulging canvas sack.

"I'm afraid they haven't been laundered," he said apologetically.

"That's perfect! That is," Frankie amended quickly, "I'm sure Miss Lamont won't mind."

She thanked him as profusely as she dared without arousing suspicion, then carried her prize outside to Russ's squad car, where the young policeman sat impatiently drumming his thumbs against the steering wheel.

"Jeepers creepers!" he exclaimed. "What are you up to now?"

Frankie tugged open the drawstring and rifled through the sack. At last she located a once-crisp white cotton shirt. She held it up by the shoulder seams, displaying the greenish-brown stains liberally spattered across the front.

"There! Smell that!"

Russ wrinkled his nose in distaste, but obediently sniffed at the stained fabric.

"Well?" Frankie demanded.

"I'd say it was some kind of herbal concoction."

"Exactly! Arthur Cohen drank some kind of herbal tea for his stomach, and his brother knew it."

Kincaid gave an exasperated sigh. "So what? My grandmother swears by chamomile and honey. Says it calms her nerves."

"Is she still living?"

"Yep. She'll be eighty-three next August."

"That's more than poor Arthur Cohen can say." Seeing Russ was not impressed, she hurried on. "Maurice didn't even have to be present to knock his brother off; all he had to do was slip something into the canister, and the next time Arthur drank his daily dose—*bang*! He's—he's—*achoo*!"

"*Gesundheit*."

"Thank you." Frankie fumbled in her purse for a handkerchief, and dabbed at her nose. "It's that herbal stuff. It makes me sneeze. But that's nothing to what it did to poor Arthur Cohen."

Russ heaved a sigh. "Look, I know you're a good kid, and your heart's in the right place. If I take this stuff and have our boys in the lab I.D. it, will you *please* give it a rest?"

Frankie was all smiles. "Oh Russ, would you do that?"

Russ raised a finger in warning. "If I do, will you quit playing detective?"

"But what if it turns out to be poison?"

"If it turns out to be poison—which I doubt—the police will take it from there."

With this Frankie was forced to be content. Russ dropped her off at the Studio Club, and she entered the common room to find Roxie, clad in a man's sweat suit of gray jersey, stretched out on the floor doing slimming exercises. The redheaded girl sat up at her entrance.

"Hey, Frankie, where's Kathleen? You didn't lose her at the cemetery, did you?"

Frankie shook her head. "She got a better offer. I take it she hasn't made it back yet?"

"Nope—two—three—four." She leaned forward to touch her toes. "Haven't seen hair nor hide of her."

"How long does it take to drink an ice cream soda, anyway?" Frankie muttered, starting up the stairs.

"What did you say?"

"I said, 'Do you have any plans for the rest of the day?' " Frankie shoved Mitch and Kathleen and their shared soda to the back of her mind. "What to catch a movie? There's a new Clark Gable picture at Grauman's."

Roxie, now on her feet, bent deeply from the waist and looked up at Frankie from between her legs. "Sorry, maybe another time." She gave Frankie an upside-down grin. "I'm going to a gramophone dance at the YMCA with a dreamboat named Harry."

"Some girls have all the luck," Frankie grumbled in mock indignation before scampering up the remaining stairs.

Upstairs, she fitted her key into the lock and opened the door. The room was dark, as she'd expected. She switched on the light and found a little pile of letters on the floor. Someone—probably Roxie—had collected her mail and pushed it underneath the door. Frankie picked it up and thumbed through the correspondence, keeping those addressed to her and tossing Kathleen's onto the other girl's bed. Her spirits lifted somewhat at the sight of her mother's handwriting; sometimes her father tucked a fiver inside. With the fate of *The Virgin Queen* in limbo, she could certainly use the money. She put the letter aside to save for last.

There was one letter addressed to "Occupant" trying to sell her a set of encyclopedias, and one for Kathleen from someone with the improbable name of Harvey Mudd. It bore a West Virginia postmark, which surprised Frankie. She didn't know Kathleen had any American acquaintances outside Hollywood. Now that she thought of it, Frankie couldn't remember her roommate ever getting any letters from relatives in England, either. Maybe they couldn't afford the expensive air mail postage or maybe her family, like Mama, disapproved of

Kathleen's ambitions. Frankie decided it was better not to ask, since it might be a sore point. She kicked off her shoes, peeled off her stockings, and curled up on the bed to read the latest news from home.

This was not all joy. Not only was there no five-dollar bill from her father, but Mama was full of the news that Charlie Compton, that nice boy who had escorted Frankie to her high school's senior prom, had come home last weekend from the University of Georgia and announced his engagement to that Thompson girl who everyone knew dyed her hair. The wedding was set for December. This was related in a slightly accusatory tone, as if it were somehow Frankie's fault and could have been avoided, had she been home to prevent it.

10

Shall We Dance (1937)
Directed by Mark Sandrich
Starring Fred Astaire and Ginger Rogers

The next morning Frankie had the Studio Club all to herself, since most of her housemates were out earning their living. The lucky ones were off acting in bit parts or even minor speaking roles; the less fortunate, attending endless casting calls or, worst of all, waiting tables. Bored with her own company, Frankie wandered into the common room where the large wooden-cased radio held pride of place. She clicked on the knob and turned up the volume.

"—Cream of Wheat is so good to eat—"

Frankie made a face and twiddled the tuning knob.

"—*Ma Perkins*, brought to you by Oxydol—"

Another tweak of the knob brought her to the CBS station.

"—*The Romance of Helen Trent*, who sets out to prove that because a woman is thirty-five, romance in life need not be over—"

Frankie heaved a sigh of annoyance that the very mention of romance should bring Mitch Gannon to mind. There was absolutely no reason why she should cling to the possibility that Kathleen's letter had been from a previously unmentioned beau back East. Just because Mitch had kissed her once on a train, it didn't mean they were a couple. Kisses these days didn't mean anything at all. Just look at the movies: actors and actresses who couldn't stand one another in real life kissed with reckless abandon on the silver screen. Things had been different in Mama's day, of course; back then, a kiss was tantamount to a proposal of marriage. But everything had changed since the War, and people were more sophisticated about such things now. Still, sometimes Frankie couldn't help wondering if the new sophistication was really such an improvement.

She switched off the radio and picked up a tattered copy of *Variety* magazine. She flipped idly through the pages, pausing here and there to admire the glossy black-and-white photographs of Fred Astaire and Ginger Rogers or Jimmy Stewart and Jean Arthur, and wondering which of her housemates had torn out the picture of Errol Flynn that was supposed to be on page fourteen. She skimmed the articles detailing upcoming productions, until one item caught her attention.

"—Worldwide Studios announced Tuesday that filming will begin next week on *The Hawk and the Dove*. A swashbuckling costume drama set in Elizabethan England, the picture has a budget of almost two million—"

Frankie gasped, unable to believe her own luck. What were the chances that another studio was about to produce a film that so closely paralleled her only real acting experience? She flipped the magazine closed and checked the date on the front cover. It was last week's issue, which meant that "next week" in the article meant this week in real time.

She hadn't a moment to lose. Clasping the glossy publication to her chest, she leaped up from her chair and clattered up the stairs to her room. She descended half an hour later, clad in a floral georgette dress and a wide-brimmed picture hat which, she hoped, would conceal the fact that she hadn't taken the time to set and style her hair. At the foot of the stairs, she rummaged through her handbag in search of loose coins. There were not as many of these as she would have liked, but she decided to splurge on a taxi anyway. It would be quicker than taking the bus, and time was of the essence.

"Worldwide Studios," Frankie instructed the driver as she climbed into the back seat. "And step on it!" She'd always wanted to say that.

The cabbie needed no further encouragement. The ride that followed was the longest twenty minutes of Frankie's life. Clutching the edge of the seat for support, she watched as the needle on the speedometer crossed forty. As it approached fifty, she closed her eyes and prayed silently for deliverance. With a screech of brakes, the taxi finally lurched to a stop.

"Here you are, Worldwide Studios."

With shaking fingers, Frankie counted out the fare and breathed a sigh of relief as she watched the cabbie drive away. Then she squared her shoulders and followed the same procedure she'd practiced so many times before since arriving in California.

"Good morning," she told the receptionist at the front desk. "My name is Frances Foster, and I'm an actress. I saw in *Variety* that Worldwide is starting to film a costume picture. I was working on *The Virgin Queen* over at Monumental, and now that filming there is in hiatus, I wondered if there might be a place for me here."

The receptionist had that "don't call us, we'll call you" expression on her face, but at the mention of Monumental Pictures something sparked in her eyes. "Straight down the hall, third door on the right."

Frankie followed the receptionist's directions and soon

found herself in a large room filled with actors and actresses of all ages, all of whom had apparently seen the same magazine article that she had. Glancing around the room, she recognized several cast members from *The Virgin Queen*. Seated along the opposite wall—and looking strangely out of character in a modern double-breasted suit and gray fedora—was the actor who had played William Cecil, and who had pronounced Arthur Cohen dead. In the far corner lurked two of her fellow serving wenches. They looked up at her entrance, then averted their eyes as if they had been caught in some shameful act.

A second door flew open, and a tall, powerfully built man regarded the company with a sneer.

"Take a look at this, Herb," he called over his shoulder. "Rats every one of 'em, rats deserting a sinking ship."

Toying with the gold chain of his pocket watch, he strolled forward to stand before William Cecil.

"Fancy meeting you here, Jim! Where were you when I wanted you to play Cardinal Wolsey? Your agent wouldn't even return my calls six months ago."

"As I told you at the time, I was under contract to Monumental," the actor replied with quiet dignity.

"And yet here you are. Contracts aren't what they used to be, are they?" The producer shook his head in mock disbelief.

"The future of the picture is still in doubt. Even if Maury

decides to continue filming, I would still be available to work for you, since most of my scenes are already in the can."

"How convenient for you." He scanned the rest of the company. "What about the rest of you?"

"We've got to find *some* way to make a living!" cried one of the serving wenches, close to tears. "How will I pay my rent?"

"Honey, you can peddle it in the street, for all I care. Old Artie knew I had an Elizabethan picture in the pipeline when he bought the script to *The Virgin Queen*. If he chose to work himself into an early grave trying to rush his film into theaters first, that's his problem. I don't feel any obligation to hire his castoffs—whether or not they had a contract."

With this pronouncement, he left the room through the same door he had entered it, shutting it behind him with enough force to rattle the windows. The members of the Monumental cast sat there for a moment in dispirited silence, then rose to their feet and shuffled toward the exit. As Frankie reached the front door, one of her fellow serving wenches fell into step beside her.

"You're an extra in the tavern scene, aren't you? I thought I recognized you. My name is Patsy Miller. There's another one of us here, too, Melinda Buford. Here she comes now."

Introductions were made all around, then Frankie and her

fellow serving wenches plodded down the sidewalk to the nearest bus stop.

"Well," Melinda declared brightly, "I thought that sounded pretty promising, didn't you?"

The other two girls stared at her in disbelief.

"Correct me if I'm wrong," Patsy said, "but I seem to recall that he recommended you give prostitution a try."

"Yes, but I'm sure he didn't mean that," she insisted with what Frankie felt was unwarranted optimism. "But the fact that he thought of sex at all just goes to show that he found me attractive, and that's half the battle, right?"

Patsy shrugged. "If you say so. It looks like I'll be going back to taxi dancing for awhile."

"What's that?" asked Frankie.

"You've never heard of taxi dancing? You know—ten cents a dance?"

Frankie's eyes grew wide. "You dance with men for money?"

"You make it sound like something dirty! It's nothing of the kind. In fact, there are bouncers on hand if the fellows cause any trouble." Seeing Frankie was not convinced, she added, "The pay is pretty good, especially on the weekends, and since I only work in the evenings, it leaves my days free for auditions. The Starlight Ballroom is looking for dancers, if you're interested."

Frankie shouldn't have even considered it. Mama would be appalled at the very idea, and Daddy probably wouldn't be wild about it, either. But her cash supply seemed to be dwindling at an alarming rate, and who knew when—or even if—filming on *The Virgin Queen* would resume.

She took a deep breath. "I guess it wouldn't hurt to give it a try."

Which explained how, at nine o'clock that evening, Frankie found herself being dragged around the dance floor in the enthusiastic, if not entirely sober, embrace of a sailor on shore leave. And to think she'd worried that her puff-sleeved, pink satin frock—a relic from her high school prom—might appear unsophisticated to the point of gaucherie among these cosmopolitan Californians. Cosmopolitan! She doubted if her partner would have noticed if she'd danced naked on the table. The same would *not* have been true of his predecessors, a boisterous trio of undergraduates from UCLA, who had descended upon the club flashing a wad of bills and paying rowdy court to all the prettiest girls until George the bouncer had threatened to toss them into the street. But even they had been an improvement over the sad sack who'd expounded at great length on how his wife didn't understand him, while trying to stroke Frankie's derriere, all to the tune of "Embraceable You."

In fact, the only thing that made the evening endurable was the pleasant weight of the coins in her tiny beaded evening bag. She hadn't had a chance to count these yet; she was proving to be very popular as a partner, and wasn't quite sure whether to feel flattered or insulted by this discovery.

At last the fruity tenor at the microphone warbled to a close, and Frankie took a hasty step backwards, out of her partner's embrace.

"That wash—was swell," he said, enunciating carefully. "Want to give it another go?"

"Thanks, but I'd better sit down and rest for a minute." She wouldn't get paid for sitting one out, but Frankie was almost certain she was rubbing a blister on her toe.

"I'll go see if I can scare us up something to drink," offered her partner, jerking his thumb in the direction of the bar.

"That would be lovely."

Privately, Frankie thought he'd had quite enough to drink already, but if she was lucky, maybe he would forget where he'd left her. She waited until he disappeared into the throng of dancers (mostly male) headed for the bar, then found a vacant spot at one of the small tables ringing the dance floor. The light cast by big rotating mirrored ball scarcely reached the dim perimeter, and Frankie took advantage of the relative privacy to pull off her silver sandal and rub her aching foot. Yes, there was definitely a raw spot beginning to form on her little toe.

"What's up, Frankie?" asked Patsy, emerging from the darkness in a shimmery ice blue number that made Frankie despise her virginal pink all the more. "Popeye the Sailor Man stepping on your feet?"

"No, I have to acquit him of that much," Frankie said, giving credit where credit was due. "He might even be a pretty good dancer if he was sober. But I rubbed a blister on my toe. All I want to do is sit here and rest my feet."

"Better not get too comfortable," Patsy said with a grin. "A fellow was asking for you earlier."

"For me? He asked for me by name?"

"Mm-hmm. He wasn't bad looking, either."

It could only mean one thing: Mitch had found out about her new job. Frankie hadn't told him, since she still wasn't entirely convinced that it was as respectable as Patsy claimed. One of the girls at the Studio Club must have told him where to find her—Kathleen, maybe, or Roxie. Or Pauline. The thought of the Studio Club's resident *femme fatale* knowing about her new job made Frankie cringe. And what about Mitch? Would he tease her about it, or would he decide she was not a nice girl after all, and try to take liberties? Frankie wasn't quite sure what sort of liberties boys took with bad girls, but they must be truly dreadful, if they couldn't even be spoken of. And yet it sometimes seemed to Frankie that bad girls had more fun than their nicer counterparts. Take Pauline, for instance. The other girls at the Studio Club hinted that Pauline was not a nice girl, and yet she had more dates and fancier dresses than anyone else there.

"Here he comes now," Patsy said, looking at someone over Frankie's shoulder. "Introduce me, why don't you?"

Frankie turned, but the figure emerging through the haze of candlelight and cigarette smoke was not Mitch. In fact, she didn't recognize the young man in the dark double-breasted suit until he reached her table.

"Officer Kincaid, is that you?" She held out her hand in greeting. "I almost didn't recognize you out of uniform."

He took her hand and gave it a squeeze. "Call me Russ, remember? As for the suit, well, joints like this aren't exactly crazy about having cops hanging around. Not that I know of anything illegal going on at the Starlight," he added quickly, seeing her alarmed expression. "It makes 'em nervous, though—a holdover from Prohibition, I guess."

"Are you on duty, then?"

"Not strictly speaking. I had some information for you, though, and one of the girls at your boarding house said I'd find you here."

Frankie was dying to find out what Russ had to say, but a sharp poke in the ribs reminded her of her social obligations. "Patsy, I'd like you to meet Russ Kincaid one of L.A.'s finest. Russ, this is Patsy Miller. She and I are both extras at Monumental."

"Another actress, huh?" Russ observed, eyeing Patsy admiringly. "Maybe when I've finished talking to Miss Foster, you'd care to dance with me?"

"Ooo, I'd be afraid to say no to a policeman." She gave Russ a wink, then moved off in search of paying partners.

"Won't you sit down?" Frankie said, gesturing toward one of the fragile bentwood chairs. "You said you had information for me?"

He sat down in the chair she indicated, but drummed his fingers on the tabletop for a moment before speaking. "It's about those stains on Arthur Cohen's shirt. The lab report came back."

"And?" Frankie prompted, leaning closer.

"And they turned out to be pennyroyal."

"Pennyroyal?" She had been hoping for arsenic or cyanide. Disappointed, she sagged in her chair. "What's that?"

"It's an herb. It has certain medicinal uses, but an overdose can kill."

"Then I was right!" she cried, all eagerness once more. "He was poisoned!"

"Whoa, whoa, hold your horses!" Russ protested, holding up a restraining hand. "You were right in that Arthur Cohen probably didn't die of a stroke or a heart attack, but it's a big jump to say he was murdered. You said yourself that he drank some herbal concoction to settle his stomach, didn't you? Who's to say he didn't brew it too strong and accidentally overdose?"

Frankie considered the possibility, her brow furrowed in concentration. "But that doesn't make sense. If he drank that concoction every day, surely he knew just how much to use, or he would have accidentally poisoned himself years ago."

"Maybe he was distracted. You said yourself he was arguing with his brother. A moment's inattention is all it would take."

"But—"

"But enough about Arthur Cohen," Russ said firmly, giving her a disarming smile. "This place is a dance hall, isn't it? What do you say we dance?"

"What's the matter, Frankie? Is this fellow bothering you?"

Frankie looked over her shoulder to find Mitch standing there wearing a dark suit and an expression like that of a bulldog guarding a bone. "Hi, Mitch. You remember Officer

Kincaid. He was just bringing me the latest news on Arthur Cohen."

The two young men shook hands, scowling at each other with mutual dislike.

"And having finished that," Russ added, "I was just asking Miss Foster to dance."

"I'm afraid you're too late," Mitch said. "All her dances are taken."

"That's ridiculous!" Frankie gestured toward the roll of tickets she wore around her wrist like a bangle. "I've still got plenty of—"

"Not anymore." Mitch slapped a bill down on the table. Abraham Lincoln gazed serenely up at them from the sleekly polished surface.

"*Five dollars?*" Frankie squeaked. "Have you lost your mind?"

"Not yet," Mitch answered cryptically, pulling out her chair as the orchestra struck up the opening bars of "Stardust." His hand at her waist, he steered her toward a vacant spot along the edge of the crowded dance floor.

"So," Frankie began, trying to ignore the little shiver that ran through her as he took her in his arms, "do you come here often?"

Mitch grinned. "Only when I'm looking for you. That

redhead back at the Studio Club—what's her name?"

"Roxie?"

"Yeah, she's the one. She told me I'd find you here. Frankie, what gives? This doesn't seem like the kind of job you would go for."

"It pays the rent," she said defensively, thankful to have something to take her mind off the warmth of his hand against the small of her back. "I've got to do *something* while Maurice is making up his mind whether to finish shooting the film."

"If you're short on funds, I could loan you—"

"No!" Mama had always said a lady shouldn't take money from a man, hinting that the man in question would expect some vague yet terrible repayment. Frankie couldn't see Mitch making inappropriate demands, but she suspected her mother was right in principle. "It's sweet of you to offer," she added in a more moderate tone, "but I don't need it. I'll pay my own way, or go back home to Georgia."

Mitch gave her a skeptical look. "Maybe so, but—a dime-a-dance girl? I don't like it."

Frankie didn't particularly like it, either, but she wasn't about to admit as much to Mitch, especially when it was all too tempting to dump her problems on his broad shoulders. "Well, who asked you, anyway? You're not my father!"

"I'm well aware of that, thank you."

"It's not that bad, really. The pay is better than waiting tables, and working at night leaves my days free for auditions." The argument had sounded perfectly logical when Patsy had made it, yet Frankie found it hard to meet Mitch's disapproving gaze. "If you're worried about the men, you shouldn't be. They're not allowed to get fresh."

"And if they try anything, Dick Tracy there will give 'em a knuckle sandwich," Mitch said dryly, jerking his head toward the table where Russ sat talking to Patsy.

"Don't tell me you're jealous of Russ!"

"Me? Jealous of him? Don't make me laugh," Mitch scoffed, even as his arm tightened possessively about her waist. "He just doesn't strike me as the kind of fellow who would hang out in a joint like this."

"He's not. He came to tell me the results of the lab tests on Arthur Cohen's shirt."

"Yeah?" Mitch's eyebrows rose. "What did they find?"

"Pennyroyal!" announced Frankie with some satisfaction.

"Who's she?"

"Not *who*, silly! *What*! It's some kind of plant."

Before she could elaborate, she was interrupted by a smattering of applause as the band played the final bars. Frankie stepped backwards out of Mitch's arms, but his fingers closed around her wrist.

"Hey, where are you going? I'm sure you're a swell dancer, but surely you don't think that was worth five bucks."

Now it was Frankie's turn to be surprised. "Surely you didn't really want to buy five dollars worth of dances! At ten cents a dance, that's—that's—" Doing math in her head was never Frankie's strong suit, and with Mitch standing so near, she found it impossible.

"Fifty dances," the recent engineering graduate informed her.

"We'll still be here dancing at closing time," she complained.

"Yeah." Mitch grinned crookedly. "That's the idea."

Frankie wasn't entirely comfortable with the idea of devoting her dances exclusively to Mitch. In fact, she had a nagging feeling that she was coming to rely too much on him, and in that doing so she might be flirting with the very fate she had traveled three thousand miles to avoid. She only had to look to her two older sisters' examples to know that moonlight and roses eventually turned into daylight and dishes. Nothing could be more fatal to a budding Hollywood career than a jealous boyfriend—and Mitch did not strike Frankie as the type who would accept with equanimity the idea of his girl shooting love scenes with another man. But for now, the night was young and the music was mellow, and Mitch seemed a far better alternative than any of the other men, most of them in various stages of intoxication, scoping out the girls in the hopes of snagging a partner for the next number.

Frankie squared her shoulders. "All right. Let's dance."

And so they did. They danced until the candles sputtered and the flowers wilted, until one by one the male clients all called it a night and went home. They danced as a sultry blonde in a low-cut black sequined gown cooed "You Made Me Love You," and an exhausted Frankie drooped bonelessly against her partner's broad chest. Mitch, never slow to seize his opportunity, put his hand on the crown of Frankie's head and tipped it forward onto his shoulder. She made no protest, but closed her eyes and made a little noise reminiscent of a kitten purring. They were still dancing when the clean-up crew began clearing the tables and the night manager announced closing time.

"How are you getting home?" Mitch asked, following Frankie as she limped from the ballroom.

She blinked like someone coming out of a trance. "What?"

"Home," Mitch repeated. He would have liked to take the credit for her bemused state, but he suspected it owed more to exhaustion than to his animal magnetism. "The Studio Club, where you live. How are you getting back there?"

"Oh," said Frankie, pushing her hair out of her eyes. "I guess I'll call a cab."

Mitch frowned. "I think I'd better give you a lift instead. It's mighty late for a girl to be out on her own."

"Oh Mitch, would you? That would be swell."

He led her out to the parking lot where he'd left his car and opened the passenger door. She collapsed onto the seat with a groan while he slid behind the wheel and turned the key in the ignition.

"Self-starter," he pointed out proudly. "No more hand cranking for me! Not if I'm going to get Cinderella home from the ball in time."

"Don't bother. Midnight was hours ago, and my stockings have already turned into rags. If I never have to wear high heels again, it'll be all too soon."

As Mitch made the turn onto Sunset Boulevard, Frankie kicked off her shoes and propped one foot up on the dashboard to inspect the damage. Mitch had always thought he was a breast man, but he took one glance at Frankie's bare toes poking through the runs in her ruined stockings and almost drove into a telephone pole.

"Soak them in Epsom salts," he recommended briskly, fixing his eyes firmly ahead. "That should toughen them up."

"My stockings?" asked Frankie, puzzled.

"No, your feet." He nodded at them without taking his eyes from the road. "We did it all the time at A & M."

"Oh." Frankie wasn't quite sure how she felt about spending over two hours held closely in a man's arms, only to have him compare her to a linebacker.

There was hardly any traffic on the streets at this late hour, and the trip back to the Studio Club was accomplished in record time. Mitch drew up next to the curb and walked Frankie to the front door. His next move presented a dilemma. Did spending five bucks for exclusive rights to dance with one particularly troublesome female qualify as a date? Did it entitle him to claim a goodnight kiss? On the other hand, even if she wasn't willing, she was probably too tired to fight him off. He might never get a better chance.

He steered her under the triple arches fronting the building to a darkened corner where the halo from the corner streetlight didn't quite penetrate. His hands closed around her shoulders, and he was just about to bend his head to kiss her when the sputter of an engine broke the silence, and the twin beams of a vehicle's headlights swung a bright arc around the corner. A moment later a milk truck drove past, the glass bottles in the back clinking together with every bump in the road.

"Mitch?" Frankie asked breathlessly.

"Yeah?"

"Will you take me to the library tomorrow?"

"I'll take you anywhere you want to go," he promised, and

lowered his head to hers.

"*Pssst!*"

Mitch snapped to attention. "What the—?"

A blond head, silver in the streetlights, leaned out of a second-floor window above their heads.

"*Pssst*! Frankie! Up here!"

"Kathleen!" Frankie exclaimed, hastily pushing Mitch away. "What are you doing up at this hour?"

"Waiting for you. You can't get in that way. The front door's locked. You'll have to go 'round to the back. I slipped down and left it on the latch for you."

"Thanks, Kathleen. You're a pal!"

"Left it on the latch?" Mitch echoed, at a loss.

"Left the back door unlocked," Frankie translated. "She's British, remember?"

"How could I forget?" He glared up at their chaperone, who apparently had no intention of leaving her post until Frankie was safely inside. "Yeah," he muttered under his breath. "A real pal."

He followed Frankie as far as the wrought iron gate at the end of the building, but before he could make another move in her direction, she had already slipped inside.

"Goodnight, Mitch," she said, looking back at him between the decorative iron bars. "You're a pretty swell guy, you know that?"

He watched as she turned and stole through the shadows to the back door. "Honey," he muttered, "you don't know the half of it."

11

Another Fine Mess (1930)
Directed by Hal Roach
Starring Stan Laurel and Oliver Hardy

True to his word, Mitch arrived at the Studio Club at ten o'clock the following morning and drove Frankie to the Hollywood branch of the Los Angeles Public Library. He'd done his homework well, and had no trouble locating the building on the corner of Hollywood Boulevard and Ivar Street. Parking along the street in the shadow of its corner tower, he found its Mediterranean façade not unlike that of the Hollywood Studio Club, with the same arched windows and doors and roof of red clay tiles. If the ornately scrolled windows looking down from the third floor of the tower had actually offered a view of the Riviera, as their architecture suggested, it would have been a promising spot to take any girl. As it was, filling such a fanciful structure with shelves of dusty books seemed to him a bit like false advertising. He could only be glad none of his teammates from A & M were here to see him. If they knew he'd sunk to taking girls to the library, he'd never live it down.

He glanced over at the passenger seat where Frankie sat, cool and crisp in a green skirt and white blouse. "Tell me again, what are we looking for?"

"I'm not sure, but I'll know it when I see it," she said, with all the confidence of a young woman on a mission. "In the meantime, we're going to learn all we can about pennyroyal."

Mitch rolled his eyes heavenward. "I can hardly wait."

Still, he followed her up the shallow stairs without protest and waited patiently while she consulted with the librarian. Minutes later, they had taken possession of a scarred wooden table in a corner, each with a stack of reference books in front of them. Mitch took the top one off the pile and began to thumb through it.

"Pennyroyal, huh?"

"Shh!" Frankie spoke in a stage whisper, one finger raised to her pursed lips. "Remember, you're in a library."

How could he forget? He looked at Frankie's invitingly puckered lips and suppressed a groan of sheer frustration. Ever since he'd kissed her on the train, he'd been looking for an opportunity—or an excuse—to do it again. But kissing in a library was probably just as forbidden as talking, and at any rate, Frankie wasn't interested. She had already turned back to her stack of books.

"Here's something," she said, ignoring her own admonition of silence. "It says here that although its effectiveness has not been proven, pennyroyal has been used for treating asthma, indigestion, liver disease, stomach disorders, and—" She looked up from the book she was reading. "Mitch, what's an abortifacient?"

"*What?*"

"Oh, am I not pronouncing it correctly? It says here that pennyroyal is sometimes used as an aborti—"

"Never mind!" Mitch put up his hands as if to ward off an attack. "I heard you the first time."

"So what is it?"

Mitch cleared his throat and ran his finger inside his collar that suddenly felt too tight. "Well, you see, when a girl does something she shouldn't—with a guy, I mean, and they're not married—" He glanced wildly about the room, desperate for some obliging librarian to shush him, but to no avail. Where were the old biddies when you needed them? "—Well, when that happens, sometimes she finds herself in trouble, and—"

Frankie gave a world-weary sigh. "I'm not stupid, Mitch. When Veronica Beauregard took up with that no-good Leroy

Lester and then got shipped off to her aunt in Richmond for six months, everybody at school knew exactly what was going on."

"Okay," Mitch said, glad to be spared the necessity of giving a lecture on the birds and the bees. "But sometimes if a girl has nowhere to go, and if the fellow won't marry her, then she has to find a way to get rid of it."

"Can you do that?" asked Frankie, wide eyed.

"Well, there are ways—apparently pennyroyal is one of them—to make it come too early—*way* too early."

"And so the baby dies?"

"It's not yet developed enough to live. It doesn't even look like a baby yet. Or so I've been told," he added hastily, lest she get the wrong impression. Heaven knew he was no saint, but he'd never gotten a girl in the family way—at least not to his knowledge.

Frankie stared thoughtfully into space. "What an awful decision to have to make."

"Dangerous, too." Mitch thought of one of his teammates from high school, who'd had to quit the football team in order to get an after-school job to pay for his girlfriend's abortion, only to have her bleed to death following the procedure. "A botched abortion can be fatal."

Frankie gave him a mischievous smile. "At least we can be certain *that* wasn't what Mr. Cohen was taking it for! He said something to his brother about indigestion, and his wife mentioned him recommending some doctor to others at the studio, but I don't remember the man's name." Her brow puckered as she considered the matter. "It seems odd that a doctor would tell him to take pennyroyal. You'd think a doctor would recommend Carter's Little Liver Pills or something like that."

"You're right," Mitch agreed, much struck. "And if a doctor did tell him to drink that stuff, surely he would have told him how much to use so he wouldn't give himself an accidental overdose."

"That's what I told Russ! I don't think Mr. Cohen accidentally poisoned himself at all. Someone else must have brewed it for him, or doctored it up somehow so that he would make it too strong."

"That would make Brother Maurice the most likely suspect. He was right there in the room with him."

Frankie shook her head. "That's what I thought too, at first, but now I'm not so sure. Maurice was scolding his brother for drinking it, remember? Why would he do that, if he wanted him to drink the poison and die?"

"That's easy. He didn't want old Artie to suspect he was up to something." Seeing Frankie was not convinced, he added, "Let's face it, Frankie, he had a motive and an opportunity. Isn't that what they always look for in the crime flicks?"

"Hmm." Frankie drummed her fingers on the table as she considered the possibilities. "So what we need to do is make a list of all the people with a reason to want Mr. Cohen dead. Then if we could somehow make a list of the people Mr. Cohen saw that day, we could compare the two."

"A list? How many enemies do you think old Artie had?"

"I don't know, but I think I met one of them yesterday. Worldwide Studios is making a picture awfully similar to Monumental's. Several of Monumental's people were there, and the producer seemed to enjoy seeing all of us begging for work. He said Arthur Cohen drove himself into an early grave trying to get his picture into theaters first. I got the impression they might've had words over it." Her face fell. "I wish I'd taken a closer look at his desk calendar that night while we were in his office. It might have given us some hint, but it's too late now."

Something about Frankie's downcast expression made Mitch want to go out and slay dragons. "You want a look at his calendar? I'll get you in there," he declared, jabbing his thumb into his chest.

"Thanks, but no thanks. Our last attempt at breaking and entering didn't work out so well, if you'll remember. I've sworn off a life of crime."

"Who said anything about breaking and entering? We'll go

there during regular office hours, I'll create a diversion, and bang! You're in."

"What kind of diversion?" Frankie asked, unconvinced.

He gave her a wink. "You just leave that to me."

"But even if it works, what makes you think the desk calendar will still be there? Surely Mr. Cohen's office has been cleaned out by this time."

"Are you kidding? There's hardly anybody at the studio these days. The place is a mausoleum."

Frankie wrinkled her nose. "That's an awful comparison to make, under the circumstances, but I see what you mean. So when do we put this plan of yours into action?"

Mitch pushed his chair back from the table and stood up. "You know what they say: there's no time like the present."

"Now?" asked Frankie, taken aback. "You mean, right this minute?"

"Are you going to chicken out on me?"

"Me, chicken? Never!" She hastily piled the books into a stack for the librarian to reshelf, then shoved her chair back. "Let's go."

Abandoning the library, they climbed back into Mitch's car and headed for the Monumental Pictures studio, stopping along the way at a service station on Hollywood Boulevard.

"Eighteen cents a gallon," Mitch grumbled. "Just watch,

it'll be up to two bits by the end of the year."

While the attendant pumped the gas and checked the oil, Mitch went inside to pay and came back with two ice-cold bottles of RC Cola and a small packet of parched peanuts.

"Drink up," he said, handing one of the bottles to Frankie.

"You didn't have to do that," Frankie began, but Mitch cut her off.

"I know I didn't have to." He tore the top corner off the packet of peanuts. "But we've got a job to do, and I want to try and catch that receptionist while most of the people in the building are at the commissary eating lunch. We might as well fortify ourselves while we've got the chance. Peanuts?"

Convinced of the logic of this argument, Frankie held out her hand, and Mitch shook half of the peanuts into her palm. The rest he poured down the narrow neck of the glass bottle, causing the soda to give off a half-hearted fizz.

Frankie watched, bemused, as he tipped the bottle up to his mouth, peanuts and all.

"It's good that way," he said defensively, seeing her dubious expression. "You ought to try it."

She shook her head. "I'll take your word for it. Now, be serious. Are you sure you can keep that receptionist occupied?"

Mitch cranked up the car and gave her a sidelong glance. "Don't you trust me?"

Frankie, at a loss for words, didn't answer. She had known many young men back home in Georgia, but Mitch wasn't like any of them. There were the nice young men that Mama expected her to marry, and there were the bad boys who got a girl in trouble and who were to be avoided at all costs. Mitch didn't seem to fit into either category. It was true that he had given her every reason to trust him; she owed her room at the Studio Club to his intervention, and his appearance at the Starlight Ballroom had been a godsend. Still, there was something about him that warned her not to get too close even though there was no real evidence against him, aside from the fact that he'd kissed her on the train and then apparently forgotten all about it, and then had gone on a date with that awful Pauline person. And Pauline still hadn't come by two o'clock in the morning. Not that Frankie was waiting up for her.

Mitch sighed and turned his attention back to his driving. "Okay, so I guess you don't trust me. How about if I promise I won't let you land in jail? Is that good enough?"

"Yes. Thank you, Mitch," Frankie said in a small voice, aware that she had hurt him without quite knowing why.

And it seemed that Mitch was as good as his word. When they reached the studio, a bored guard waved them through the gate with a lazy hand, and in no time at all they entered the Spanish-style stucco building that housed the Monumental offices. The same receptionist sat at the desk eating an apple and reading a magazine. As they entered, she hastily shut the magazine and stuffed it into the top drawer of her desk. *Photoplay*, Frankie guessed, or maybe *Modern Screen*.

"I'm sorry to interrupt your lunch," Frankie said pleasantly. "I was just wondering if there was any news on when they might resume filming on *The Virgin Queen*." She could feel her face grow warm, and deplored the necessity of mentioning the V-word in front of Mitch.

"Not that I know of." the receptionist looked at them over the top of her glasses. "The only one who might know is Maurice Cohen, and he's not telling."

"Could I see him?" Frankie tried to sound hopeful, knowing quite well that, at this time, he would be out to lunch. At least, she hoped he was out to lunch. If he happened to be spending the lunch hour in his office, all her plans would be wrecked.

"He's out to lunch right now." The receptionist toyed with the chain dangling from her glasses. "If you'd like to leave a message, I'll see that he gets it."

Frankie hesitated, looking for an excuse to linger, when Mitch spoke up.

"I could use a little lunch myself. What do you say, Frankie? My treat."

Frankie was just about to remind him that he'd just downed an entire RC Cola and most of a bag of peanuts when she saw the look he gave her.

"That sounds swell," she said quickly. "I'd like to powder my nose first, if Miss—" She glanced at the desk, where a small wooden plaque bore the name of Martha Honeycutt. "—Miss Honeycutt will point me toward the ladies' room."

Miss Honeycutt gestured toward the corridor. "Down the hall to your right, third door on the left."

"Thanks. Back in a jiffy," she added to Mitch, waggling her fingers at him.

The ladies' room was in the opposite direction from Arthur Cohen's office, but Frankie headed down the hall in that direction anyway. She stopped outside the ladies' room door, counted to ten, then tiptoed back down the hall in the other direction. As she passed the open doorway to the front office, she heard Mitch's voice.

"Honeycutt, eh? It suits you. A sweet name for a sweet girl."

"Hardly a girl, Mr.—?"

"Gannon. But you can call me Mitch."

"Mr. Gannon," the secretary said firmly, clearly holding no truck with fresh young men. "As I said, I'm no girl. I've worked for Monumental for eight years."

"You're kidding me! How come no fellow has ever come in here and carried you off?"

I think I'm going to be sick, Frankie thought, rolling her eyes as she tiptoed quickly past.

The door to Arthur Cohen's office was closed but not locked. Frankie slipped inside and allowed her eyes a moment to adjust to the dim light. She didn't dare switch on the overhead light lest someone returning from lunch notice the light underneath the door. She moved toward the big desk, her footsteps muffled by the thick carpet. Someone—removing incriminating evidence, perhaps?—had made an attempt at cleaning. Several personal items that Frankie remembered from her earlier visit were now gone, including a silver fountain pen in a stand and a framed photograph which Frankie now realized must have been a picture of Letitia Lamont. The desk calendar was also missing, so any secrets it might have contained were lost. The blotter was still there but the top sheet, which had been covered with scribblings before, was now pristine.

Or was it? Frankie knelt beside the desk and studied the blotter more closely. From this new angle, she could see indentations on the paper left by Mr. Cohen's pen on the sheet above. She had a sudden idea, and gingerly slid open the top drawer of the desk. Just as she had hoped, there was a motley collection of pencils, paper clips, and rubber bands. She took out a pencil, laid it almost flat against the blotter, and ran it lightly back and forth across the page. Just as she had hoped, words and numbers in Arthur Cohen's firm scrawl appeared, white against the gray markings of the pencil lead.

But what did they mean? A notation near the top left-hand corner read "Ruby 12:30." Was Ruby an actress to whom he'd meant to give a screen test, or had he planned to meet with a jeweler to buy gemstones for his wife? There was no way of knowing.

The middle of the paper held more promising clues. The telephone exchange "HO 7-2214" stood out clearly, as did "BR 4-1539," this last bearing the one-word heading of "Winston." It wasn't much to go on, Frankie thought, but it was a start. Back at the Studio Club, she would call both numbers and see if they yielded any useful information. She tore off the top sheet, careful not to leave incriminating fingerprints on the paper beneath. She folded the sheet three times and was just about to tuck it away into her purse when an unwelcome thought occurred to her. There was only one telephone at the Studio Club, and when it wasn't in use by one of the girls setting up auditions or job interviews, it was usually tied up by Pauline cooing suggestively to one of her admirers—a motley collection that seemed to include half the male population of California. Even if by some miracle the telephone was available, the other girls were certain to be nearby, making a private conversation all but impossible.

Her gaze drifted to the squat black telephone on the desk. Would Miss Honeycutt be able to tell if this phone was in use? Could Mitch keep her too distracted to notice? Frankie decided to chance it. She lifted the receiver from its cradle and raised it to her ear.

"Brighton four, fifteen thirty-nine," she murmured, not daring to raise her voice.

"You'll have to speak up, honey, I can't hear you," the operator's voice crackled from the other end of the line.

"Brighton four, fifteen thirty-nine," she repeated, a bit stronger this time.

"One moment." There was a pause, then a click, and a woman's voice came through the receiver.

"Dr. Winston's office. May I help you?"

In spite of her nervousness, Frankie felt a rush of triumph. A doctor! Surely he could shed some light on Arthur Cohen's health prior to his death. He might even know something about the herbal tea.

"This is Frances Foster," Frankie said, certain that the pounding of her heart could be heard all the way down the telephone line. "I'm calling on behalf of Mr. Arthur Cohen."

"You say Mr. Cohen referred you?" asked the tinny voice

on the other end of the line.

It wasn't exactly the way Frankie would have put it, but it seemed easier than making awkward explanations. "Yes," she said.

"Would you like to schedule an appointment?"

Frankie hated to take up a doctor's time when she wasn't really sick, but a scheduled visit might be the easiest way to speak to the doctor in private. "Yes, please."

"Dr. Winston can see you tomorrow at ten-thirty, if that is convenient."

"Tomorrow at ten-thirty will be fine, thank you."

Frankie hung up the receiver feeling very pleased with herself. Emboldened by success, she decided to try the second number, trusting to Mitch to cover for her until she was finished.

"Hollywood seven, twenty-two fourteen," she informed the operator, more boldly this time. She hadn't long to wait until an answering voice came through the line, this one raspy and male.

"Eddie here. What's up?"

The abruptness of the question robbed Frankie of her earlier confidence. "H-hello, Mr.—er, Eddie," Frankie stammered, "I'm calling on behalf of Mr. Arthur Cohen—"

"Yeah, I'll just bet you are," interrupted the unknown Eddie. "Look, I didn't get where I am today by falling for every dame with a sob story. It's a shame what happened to your old man, but I've got bills to pay too, you know."

"I—I'm afraid there must be some mistake—"

"There's been a mistake, all right, and poor old Artie's the one who made it. I could have told him Peg o' My Heart wouldn't finish higher than fifth."

"But—but—"

"Look, Miss Lamont, I'm a reasonable man, but I can't wait forever. You could always hock the hardware, you know. I'll bet you could get a pretty penny for old Oscar at auction. I'll even give you a tip: Hail Caesar in Saturday's two-thirty."

Frankie slammed down the telephone and pressed a shaking hand to her rib cage. This Eddie person was a gambler! So too, had Arthur Cohen been, and not a very lucky one at that. Eddie seemed to be pressing Letitia Lamont to make good on her husband's gambling losses. But who was Oscar, and what did Eddie mean about selling him at auction? Frankie thought that sort of thing had ended with the War Between the States.

Maybe Mitch would know. Frankie folded the paper and stuffed it into her purse, then retraced her steps back down the hall to where Mitch waited. To her chagrin, he didn't seem concerned about her long absence at all. In fact, he seemed to be enjoying himself hugely. He sat perched on the edge of Miss Honeycutt's desk, while the gatekeeper of Monumental Pictures (her horn-rimmed glasses mysteriously vanished) simpered and blushed like a June bride.

"Seriously," he was telling her, "you ought to be up on the silver screen yourself, instead of hidden away behind this desk."

"Oh, I'm afraid I'm too old for that," she protested, with a coy smile that encouraged Mitch to argue the point.

"Hogwash! Lots of men prefer an experienced woman. Why, I'll bet—"

"Sorry to take up so much of your time," Frankie interrupted, smiling at the pair of them through clenched teeth. "If you're ready, Mitch, we'll let Miss Honeycutt get back to her work."

"Oh, it was a pleasure, I'm sure," the secretary insisted, clutching Mitch's sleeve as if she intended to keep him there by force. "Until seven o'clock, then?"

"Seven," echoed Mitch, sounding oddly deflated.

Frankie bit her tongue until they were safely outside, but as soon as they reached the relative privacy of Mitch's car, she rounded on him.

"What the—the *heck* was that all about?" Her sense of betrayal drowned out even Mama's well-known opinion of ladies who used slang.

"Dammit, what took you so long?" demanded Mitch, who had no such qualms where language was concerned. "Another five minutes and I might have been engaged to that woman!"

179

"Funny, but you didn't seem to be suffering!"

"No, that part comes later. Seven o'clock tonight, to be exact."

"What happens at seven?" Frankie asked, curiosity overcoming indignation.

Mitch sighed. "I have a date."

Frankie's eyes grew round. "With Miss Honeycutt? But she's *years* older than you!"

"Some men prefer experienced women," Mitch repeated his own words with bitter irony.

"But if you didn't want to go out with her, why did you ask her?"

"Are you kidding? That phone of hers was blinking like a blasted traffic light. I had to do something to keep her occupied." He gave her a sidelong glance as he shifted the car into gear. "I hope it was worth it."

"Oh, it was! I found phone numbers written on Mr. Cohen's blotter, and one of them turned out to be some gambling person named Eddie. Mitch, I think Mr. Cohen had been losing a lot of money betting on racehorses!"

"Come to think of it, he told us he preferred them to team sports, remember? Go on, what else did this Eddie tell you?"

"He thought I was Mrs. Cohen, which means he's never met Letitia Lamont, because if he had, he would never mistake my voice for hers. And he intends to make her pay off her husband's gambling debts, even if she has to go to work in a hardware store."

"A hardware store?" Mitch echoed in be-wilderment. "Why would she do that? I mean, it's hard to picture a former goddess of the silent screen peddling nuts and bolts."

"I thought so, too, but that's what he said. And he said something else that struck me as strange."

"What now? Did he suggest she get a job at the dry cleaner's?"

Frankie refused to take the bait. "No, he suggested she put some man up for auction. Can people do that?"

"Who was the man, did he say?"

"Someone named Oscar."

"Aha!" exclaimed Mitch as enlightenment dawned. "Elementary, my dear Watson. You are forgetting you're not in Georgia anymore. In this town, Oscar isn't a person. He's a little gold statue of a guy holding a sword."

"That's it!" Frankie cried, bouncing on the seat in her excitement. "Letitia Lamont won an Oscar for her work in *A Brand from the Burning*. It was five or six years ago—one of the last silent films to win an Academy Award."

"I guess it would bring a pretty penny then, huh? Collectors would probably pay a fortune for a piece of movie history."

"She won a lot of other awards, too," Frankie said thoughtfully. "Do you think that was what Eddie meant by selling hardware—auctioning off her trophies and plaques and things?"

"Could be," Mitch said, not entirely convinced. "But you said he mentioned a store."

Frankie closed her eyes, trying to recreate the conversation. "Not exactly. He said she could 'hock the hardware' if she needed money."

"Don't stray from the script," Mitch scolded.

Frankie's brown eyes grew round as a memory clicked into place. "And that's exactly what she's doing!"

"What? Straying from the script?" asked Mitch, all at sea.

"No, silly! She's been selling off souvenirs. At her house I noticed big blank spots on the wall where portraits must have hung. But now that I think of it, there wasn't a picture of her in *A Brand from the Burning*, or *Another Reapeth*, or several of her other most famous roles."

"Maybe she sold the most valuable ones first, to get Eddie off her back."

"Or maybe Mr. Cohen had sold them himself, while he was still alive."

"So he'd already gambled away his own fortune, and was

starting to make dents in his wife's? Now, there's a motive for murder."

"You think Eddie killed him?" Frankie asked, baffled by his logic.

"No, Eddie would have had every reason to want him alive. But the little woman might have been displeased, to say the least."

"She didn't seem exactly prostrate with grief," Frankie admitted. "She didn't seem awfully surprised, either. She said he was under a lot of stress, with his work and all."

"Yeah, it must have been a hard way to live, having beautiful girls throwing themselves at you, begging you to make them a star," Mitch drawled.

"But if she had been at the studio that day, surely someone must have mentioned seeing her there. Besides, she couldn't have gotten into his office anyway. He already had an appointment, either with a jeweler or a woman named Ruby." She explained the cryptic note scrawled on the blotter.

"Maybe his wife *is* Ruby," Mitch suggested. "Letitia Lamont sure sounds like a stage name to me."

"It is. But according to *Picture Play*, her real name was Annie Crumb."

Mitch made a face. "I can see why she changed it."

But Frankie lost interest in the producer's wife as a new

idea occurred to her. "Mitch, you don't suppose Mr. Cohen *wanted* to die, do you?"

"Committed suicide, you mean? I don't know, Frankie, that's an awfully big leap."

"But if he'd gotten in over his head with Eddie and saw no way of getting out, it might have seemed like his only option. He'd know how to do it, too, with that stuff he drank for his stomach. He seems to have been warned about it often enough." His doctor would know, she thought. This Dr. Winston would know if Arthur Cohen had been depressed, or frightened, or just plain jumpy. Of course, he might consider that information confidential and refuse to tell her anything at all, but she would cross that bridge when she came to it.

"Maybe we should drive down to Santa Anita and ask a few questions," Mitch suggested.

"What's at Santa Anita?"

"Horseracing. I'm guessing it's where Arthur Cohen played the ponies."

"A racetrack?" Frankie's wide brown eyes grew troubled. "I don't know, Mitch, Mama doesn't approve of gambling."

"Mama won't know unless you tell her," he pointed out. "How about tomorrow morning? Pick you up at ten?"

"It's a good idea, Mitch, really it is, but I can't." Seeing the knowing grin he cast in her direction, she added quickly, "It's not because of Mama. I have an appointment tomorrow, that's all."

The large Mediterranean bulk of the Studio Club loomed up on the right, and Mitch wheeled up to the curb and braked to a stop. Frankie, climbing out on the passenger side, was surprised to see Mitch sliding from beneath the wheel, clearly intending to walk her to the door.

"I wish I could invite you in, but I need to wash my hair before I go to work. Maybe you could come by the Starlight Ballroom tonight and we could make plans for going to Santa Anita another day."

Mitch grimaced. "I've already got plans. I have a date tonight, remember?"

"Oh, that's right. I forgot." She felt a pang of envy for Mitch, who at worst would spend a couple of hours at a movie theater with an overeager spinster while she, Frankie, would be dragged about the dance floor by every stage door Johnny with spare change in his pocket. Or was it the overeager spinster that she envied? No, that was ridiculous; Miss Honeycutt wouldn't have a date with Mitch at all if he hadn't been worried that her own prolonged absence might make the secretary suspicious. She should be jealous of Frankie, instead of the other way 'round. The knowledge made her grateful to Mitch and aware of her own feminine power.

"I'm sorry I dragged you into this." She laid her hand on his arm. "If it makes you feel any better, I do think I got a couple of good leads, and—and I can't think of anyone I'd rather have guarding my back."

And quickly, before she lost her nerve, she stood on tiptoe and kissed him on the cheek, then turned and hurried into the Studio Club without looking back.

12

Casanova's Big Night (1954)
Directed by Norman Z. McLeod
Starring Bob Hope, Joan Fontaine, and Basil Rathbone

Mitch prepared for his date that evening in a far more cheerful frame of mind than the occasion warranted. Frankie had kissed him. True, the kiss was inspired more by gratitude than any passion for himself, but it was a start, and all because she was grateful to him for holding Miss Honeycutt at bay—watching her back, she'd said. Well, he'd be more than happy to watch her front, too; so many of a female's best parts were located there.

He was still whistling cheerfully when he parked his car in front of the boarding house where Martha Honeycutt lived. He sauntered up the front walk, resisting the urge to jump up and click his heels together, and rang the doorbell.

The sight of his companion for the evening was enough to wipe the song from his lips. Mitch didn't know enough about women's clothing to recognize inferior cut, but even he could see that Martha Honeycutt's dress clung where it should have bloused and bloused where it should have clung. Her mousy hair had been crimped within an inch of its life, and as he drew nearer he could detect beneath her cheap perfume a faintly smoky smell, as if she had singed it with a curling iron. The horn-rimmed glasses she'd worn at work had been replaced by a gaudy pair adorned with rhinestones.

"Good evening, Mitchell," she chirped, tugging at the neckline of her ill-fitting dress. "I see you didn't have any trouble finding the house."

"Nope, none at all," Mitch said with a twinge of regret for having been denied this excuse for standing her up. "You gave good directions. Now, if you're ready, we'll be on our way."

She clutched at his sleeve. "Oh, but don't you want to step inside first?" She tittered. "The other girls are all agog to meet my new beau."

Mitch suppressed a shudder. He'd rather have a root canal. "It sounds swell, but we'd better get a move on if we want to catch the newsreel and the serial before the main feature."

Her face fell, but she allowed him to take her elbow and steer her toward the curb where his car waited. "What are we going to see?"

"*The Public Enemy* is playing at the Bijou. I missed it when it first came out a couple of years ago, but I've heard it's pretty good. Do you like James Cagney?"

"I like Clark Gable better," she said, peering up at him hopefully. "I've seen *It Happened One Night* five times."

Mitch knew for a fact that Gable's latest picture had just opened at Grauman's, but he wasn't about to suggest it. He didn't flatter himself that any woman would prefer him to the Hollywood's biggest heartthrob, but he had a sneaking suspicion that Martha Honeycutt wouldn't be too choosy about a substitute. No, a good old gangster shoot-'em-up would be safer than anything hinting of romance. In the meantime, though, there was no reason he shouldn't get what information he could out of the receptionist, thus salvaging something from an otherwise painful evening.

"Clark Gable, huh?" he said, once he had seated her in the passenger seat and taken his place behind the wheel. "I guess you've met all the big stars, working in the front office the way you do."

"Clark Gable has never come to Monumental, not that I'm aware of. Jimmy Stewart came by once, though. Mr. Cohen— Arthur, that is, not Maurice—was hoping to borrow him from MGM for some picture. Nothing came of it, though, so I never saw him again." She sighed. "It was a pity, too. He was just as nice in person as he is on the screen."

"What about Mr. Cohen's wife?" Mitch asked with studied nonchalance. "I heard she was pretty famous back in the day."

"Yes, she was a big star in the silent pictures." Martha clearly relished her role as an expert. "She's still a very attractive woman, but her voice is all wrong for sound. It's sad, really. The same thing happened to poor John Gilbert, you know, and he was the biggest thing since Valentino."

Mitch had no interest whatsoever in John Gilbert and even less in Valentino. "So Mrs. Cohen is still attractive, huh? You say that like you've seen her recently."

"Oh, Miss Lamont, as she prefers to be called, drops by the studio all the time," she assured him with an airy wave of her hand. "She's always been very kind and friendly to me."

"Was she there the day her husband died?" He saw Martha regarding him curiously through her ridiculous glasses, and realized his question had been too abrupt for casual interest. "I know she wasn't on the set at the time, but it would have been nice if they'd had a chance to say their last goodbyes."

"I don't recall seeing her that day, but now that you mention it, I remember she'd been in earlier in the week to have lunch with Mr. Cohen. He was out of the office, though, so she ate lunch with her brother-in-law instead." She lowered her voice to a stage whisper. "Arthur's loss was Maurice's gain, if you know what I mean."

Mitch's passenger-side wheels grazed the sidewalk as his gaze slewed around to the woman who sat beside him. "Are you saying Maurice Cohen—and his brother's wife—?"

"Nothing ever happened between them, at least not that I know of," Martha back-pedaled quickly and, Mitch thought, regretfully. "But he's been in love with her for years. Everyone at the studio knows that."

Mitch was willing to bet there was one person at the studio—besides himself—who didn't know, and wondered what she would make of the information. Maybe he would drop by the Studio Club in the morning and find out.

"If that's true," he said cautiously, "I guess they're free to marry now that Arthur is out of the way."

"After a decent mourning period, anyway," Martha amended. "It wouldn't look right to marry too soon after poor Mr. Arthur's death."

Privately Mitch thought that anyone capable of committing murder probably wouldn't be too squeamish about offending propriety by waiting less than the standard twelve months. Not that he knew for sure that either the brother or the wife had killed Arthur Cohen. Nor, for that matter, could he be certain that Martha wasn't exaggerating a perfectly innocent relationship; surely it wasn't unusual for women of a certain age, deprived of romance in their own lives, to make it up out of whole cloth where the lives of others were concerned, particularly when one was surrounded, as Martha Honeycutt was, by the wealthy, famous, and beautiful.

The rest of the drive passed without incident, and soon they arrived at the theater, where Mitch paid ten cents each for their admission. Once inside, the concessions counter presented a fresh dilemma. Ordinarily, Mitch bought two sodas and one large bag of popcorn for himself and his date to share: besides saving a nickel, this arrangement offered all sorts of opportunities for hands to brush. He had fond memories of one especially imaginative coed who had salvaged an uninteresting newsreel by sucking the butter from his pinky finger. The thought of Martha Honeycutt having any such notions was enough to decide him.

"Two popcorns," he told the perky young woman behind the counter, plunking down a quarter.

The seating arrangements brought problems, as well. Normally Mitch preferred to steer his date toward the darkest seats in the back row, the better for engaging in extracurricular activities should the film turn out to be a dud. Although he didn't want to give Martha the wrong idea, neither did he want to be seen with her—after all, he did have a certain reputation to uphold where the female of the species was concerned. As he paused in the aisle and scanned the available seats, his date took the decision out of his hands.

"Look, there are two seats right down front," she declared, pointing down the aisle where the seats were lit by the flickering light from the big screen. "We'll be able to see so much better there."

Heaving a sigh, Mitch followed her down the aisle, consoling himself with the knowledge that he knew hardly anyone in Los Angeles apart from the staff at the studio. With any luck, anyone seeing him and Martha together would assume he'd lost a bet.

While Mitch sat in a darkened theater, his legs pressed tightly together lest his knee accidentally brush that of his date, Frankie donned her old prom gown and prepared for her shift at the Starlight Ballroom. As she crossed the Studio Club foyer, Kathleen's clipped British accent hailed her from the common room.

"Why, Frankie! Don't you look sweet!"

Frankie paused in the doorway and saw a cluster of young actresses gathered around the radio. Several of them, Kathleen and Roxie included, darned their silk stockings as they listened to *Your Hit Parade*. Pauline sat apart from the others, shellacking her fingernails a vivid scarlet.

" 'Sweet' is the idea." Frankie plucked at her full skirts. "Fellows are less likely to take liberties with a girl who looks like her daddy is coming to pick her up at ten o'clock."

Pauline looked up from her fingernails. "Surely you can't be referring to Mitchell? Why, I found him to be a perfect gentleman."

"I'm not—"

"Frankie isn't interested in your leftovers," Roxie retorted. "It so happens she's working at the Starlight Ballroom. And I think she looks very nice."

"Maybe a bit *too* nice, darling," Pauline purred. "You might find the men tip more generously if you look a bit more— well, sophisticated. That dress might do very well in Georgia, but here in Hollywood it looks like something Mickey Rooney's date might wear to the high school dance."

She held out one red-tipped hand for inspection and, apparently satisfied with the result of her labors, jabbed the tiny brush back into the bottle, then rose and sashayed from the room.

The remaining girls stared at one another in speechless indignation. Roxie, the first to recover, leaped to her feet.

"You might find the men more generous if you look a bit more sophisticated, *dahling*," she cooed, snatching up one filmy stocking and flinging it over her shoulder like a feather boa. In her own voice, she added, "One thing's for sure, no one ever accused Pauline of being too nice."

"She's right about this dress, though," Frankie said with a sigh. "I did wear it to the high school dance."

"Was Mickey Rooney your date?" Roxie asked, to a chorus of giggles.

Frankie ignored the interruption. "But I'd rather wear my old prom dress than that black thing she wore, with the front cut down to *there*, and as for the back—"

"Pauline does have her uses, though." Roxie flopped back onto the sofa and picked up her mending. "She found a terrific store on Sunset Boulevard that sells secondhand clothes from the studio wardrobes, or even from the stars themselves. I saw a gown there last week that I'm almost positive Myrna Loy wore to the Oscars last year."

Frankie's eyes widened in mingled admiration and envy. "You got to go to the Oscars last year?"

"No, but I saw plenty of pictures in the fan magazines." She snapped her fingers as inspiration dawned. "I just had a great idea! Why don't we go there tomorrow—to the store, I mean, not the Oscars!—and look for you a dress? Surely we can find you something that won't break the bank. Kathleen can come too, to give us an air of old-world elegance."

Kathleen eagerly accepted the invitation, but Frankie shook her head. "I'm afraid I'll have to decline. I've got an appointment in the morning."

"Do tell!" Roxie leaned forward. "It isn't a screen test, is it?"

"Nothing so glamorous, unfortunately. Just a doctor's appointment."

Kathleen's English rose features took on a worried expression. "Are you ill?"

Seeing the concern in her friends' eyes, Frankie wished she hadn't volunteered quite so much information. Roxie didn't know about her suspicions regarding Arthur Cohen's death, and Kathleen kept urging her to give up playing detective. "No, it's just a consultation—assuming I can find his office, that is. Do either of you know which bus I should take to get to Dr. Henry Winston's office on North Vine?"

Roxie's stocking slipped through her fingers and fell unnoticed on her lap. Kathleen jabbed her finger with her needle, and instinctively raised the abused digit to her mouth.

"Frankie, honey," Roxie said, suddenly serious, "are you— in trouble?"

"No, but I will be if *The Virgin Queen* doesn't resume production soon. The Starlight Ballroom pays the bills, but it's not the sort of work a girl wants to do all her life."

"Sit down and tell Aunt Roxie all about it," the redhead urged, patting the sofa cushion beside her.

"I'd love to, but I can't afford to be late. If I don't see you before tomorrow, enjoy your shopping trip."

Frankie, headed for the door, didn't see the worried look the two girls exchanged behind her back.

Frankie's partners that night found her a very poor bargain, as she was so distracted with thoughts of what she might learn from Dr. Winston that she paid very little attention to any of the men who paid for the privilege of dancing the tango or foxtrot with her. One enterprising fellow, seeing her mind was elsewhere, seized the opportunity to slide his hand down from her waist and pinch her on the backside. Had Mitch been present to witness this piece of impertinence, the young man would no doubt have ended the evening with fewer teeth than he had begun it. But Mitch was busy fending off unwanted advances on his own account, and so Frankie was forced to act in her own defense—which she did by grinding her high heel into her partner's instep.

"Oh, did I do that?" she asked with exaggerated sweetness as her partner clutched his injured foot. "I'm *so* sorry!"

It was not a good night for tips, for which Frankie had only herself to blame. Even those of her partners who escaped physical damage soon abandoned her for more accommodating females. But in spite of her meager haul, Frankie decided to splurge on a taxi to Dr. Winston's office, since she was unsure of the bus route.

And so the following morning she rose, dressed in the blue suit she'd worn on the train west, and flagged down a taxi to take her to 864 North Vine. A short time later, the cab lurched to a stop in front of what appeared to be a private residence set back at a discreet distance from the road.

"Is nice place, no?" he asked in the broken English of the recent immigrant.

Reluctant to leave the cab until she was sure of her location, Frankie looked out the window at the stucco walls and clay roof tiles that seemed to adorn half the houses in California. "It's supposed to be a doctor's office. Doctor?" she added uncertainly, wondering if her accent was as foreign to his ear as his was to her. "Medico?"

He grinned, teeth flashing white against his brown face. "Ah, Doctor Winston." He pronounced it "Weenston." "He fix you up pronto." He bounded out of the cab and opened the back door with a flourish.

"Oh, thank you!" Frankie was so relieved to know she'd come to the right place, she didn't bother to correct his assumption that she was one of Dr. Winston's patients. "You've been very kind."

She paid her fare along with as generous a tip as she could spare, then turned and walked up the sidewalk to the green-painted door.

Her first impression upon entering Dr. Winston's waiting room was that it was the gloomiest place she had ever seen. Not that the furnishings were unwelcoming; in fact, the colorful rag rugs and floral chintz upholstered sofas had more in common with a cozy living room than a doctor's office. There were none of the institutional whitewashed walls and bare linoleum floors usually found in medical establishments, and only the faintest odor of Lysol to betray the building's true purpose.

The doctor's patients, however, were another thing entirely. Exclusively female, they ranged in age from the late teens to the middle thirties, and while none of them looked precisely ill, neither did any of them look happy to be there. One, an ethereal blonde who didn't look a day over sixteen, appeared to be puffy-eyed from crying. Another, this one a beautiful brunette, plucked at the folds of her skirt and stared fixedly at the floor. A tight-lipped redhead was apparently seeing the doctor for a stomach ailment, for she kept her hand pressed tightly to her abdomen. In the far corner of the room, a long-legged blonde wore dark glasses even though the curtains at the windows were tightly drawn. Something about her looked vaguely familiar, although Frankie couldn't place her.

Frankie signed in at the desk, then sank into one of the overstuffed sofas and picked up a magazine from the low table. A few moments later, an inner door opened and a nurse in a starched white dress consulted the chart in her hand.

"Mary Smith."

A movement in the far corner of the room caught Frankie's eye as the woman in the dark glasses rose in answer to the nurse's summons. Suddenly Frankie realized where she had seen the woman before. She had starred as Marie Antoinette in Worldwide Picture's remake of their silent film *Madame Guillotine*. The set of her jaw and her resolute tread as she crossed the doctor's waiting room was exactly the same as that of her royal persona as she approached the guillotine on screen. And while Frankie couldn't quite recall the actress's name, she was quite certain it was not Mary Smith.

As the women were called one by one, Frankie gradually became aware that there seemed to be a preponderance of Smiths, Joneses, and even one Jane Doe. She also became aware that none of the young women came back. She supposed there must be a rear door and wondered if this arrangement, like the false names and Marie Antoinette's dark glasses, was an effort to protect the actresses from the gossip columnists. After all, if Hedda Hopper saw a young starlet entering or leaving a doctor's office, the next installment of "Hedda Hopper's Hollywood" might have her dying of cancer.

Eventually Frankie's name was called, and she followed the nurse down a hallway to a small examining room furnished with a padded table, a single straight chair, and a glass-fronted cabinet containing an assortment of ominous-looking metal instruments. She was puzzling over the lack of diplomas on the wall—in her admittedly limited experience, doctors seemed to take great pride in the number of framed diplomas adorning the walls—when the door opened to admit the doctor. Doctor Winston was a well-fed man with an ingratiating smile that showed too many teeth. Frankie found herself uncomfortable in his presence without quite knowing why. Certainly there was nothing inherently frightening in his comportment; in fact, the man practically oozed bedside manner.

"Miss Foster, is it?" he asked, taking her hand and pressing it warmly. "Such a pretty young thing! Never fear, my dear, we'll have you fixed up in no time."

"Oh, I'm not here as a patient," Frankie objected, gently but firmly withdrawing her hand from his clasp. "I would just like to ask you a few questions about—"

"Of course, of course." Nodding reassuringly, he motioned her toward the chair. "I'll be glad to tell you anything you need to know. Although you must be aware that time is of the essence in these cases."

"Oh, I quite agree!" Frankie exclaimed in some surprise, wondering how much he had guessed about the purpose of her visit.

"Now, when did you first realize you were," he paused significantly, "in trouble?"

"As soon as I saw Mr. Cohen keel over dead," Frankie said, shuddering at the memory.

"Then he had not as yet referred you to me?" the doctor asked, jotting noted on a pad as he spoke.

"No. I got your telephone number from his office, and his wife had mentioned your name."

"Had she, now? Well, that's very generous of her, but then I suppose she's used to it by this time. Whatever his faults—and I'm sure they were inevitable, surrounded as he was by beautiful and ambitious young women such as yourself—he always took care of his girls. He has referred numerous young women to me over the years, and I have always done what I can to offer them a way out of their difficulties. His death has not changed that. The bill for my services will be sent to the studio, as usual, so the matter of money need not concern you."

Frankie's eyes had grown steadily wider during this speech. Suddenly it all made a horrible sort of sense: the discreet location, the unseen back entrance, and, worst of all, the frightened, desperate women in the waiting room.

"Then you are not—" Frankie groped for words, unwilling to accept the evidence of her own eyes. "—Not Mr. Cohen's personal physician?"

Dr. Winston chuckled, his belly shaking beneath his white lab coat. "My dear girl, Mr. Cohen must have found your innocence charming! No, my clientele is limited to young women with certain—" again that significant pause, "—female problems. Now, if you will lie down on the table, I will attempt to determine how much time we have until you begin to show. Beyond that point, I'm afraid the procedure is considerably more difficult."

Frankie's worse fears were confirmed. This was no ordinary doctor's office, but a terrible place, a place where unspeakable things happened. She leaped up from the chair and ran from the room, through the waiting room and out the door into the brilliant sunlight.

13

Damsel in Distress (1937)
Directed by George Stevens
Starring Fred Astaire, Joan Fontaine,
George Burns, and Gracie Allen

While Frankie sat in Dr. Winston's waiting room, Mitch set out on the twenty-five mile drive to Arcadia and the thoroughbred racetrack at Santa Anita Park. Opened a mere two years earlier, it was already a popular haunt of the Hollywood set, and given the late producer's self-professed weakness for horseracing, Mitch thought it highly likely that Arthur Cohen had spent a significant amount of time—and money—there. Today was not a race day, so the parking lot in front of the grandstand entrance was nearly empty. He parked his car in the shade of a cluster of palm trees near the imposing turquoise-blue façade and went inside.

After a morning spent in the brilliant California sunshine, it took a moment for his eyes to adjust to the dim light within. The grandstand area was as empty as the parking lot and Mitch's footsteps echoed in the stillness as he walked through the building and out on the other side, where it opened onto the racetrack itself and the view of the San Gabriel Mountains beyond. Here, at last, were signs of life: on the far side of the mile-long track a jockey leaned over the neck of a beautiful chestnut thoroughbred while two men watched from the railing nearby. One held a stopwatch in his hand, obviously timing the practice laps, while the other watched the horse and rider through a pair of binoculars.

It seemed as good a place as any to start. Conscious of a few butterflies in his stomach, Mitch dug in his pocket for the pack of Lucky Strikes that Frankie had so deplored. He felt a certain grudging admiration for the way she plunged headlong into this sort of situation without, apparently, a second thought. Well, if she could do it, so could he. He lit a cigarette and took a long drag, then headed toward the two men standing along the railing.

" 'Morning." He lifted one hand in a careless wave. "I'm looking for Arthur Cohen. I've heard he's a regular here. Know anything about his whereabouts?"

The two men stared at Mitch as if he'd just sprouted horns.

"Have you been living under a rock for the past week?" asked the man with the binoculars. "He's dead—had a heart attack, or maybe it was a stroke, on the movie set and died instantly, from what I hear."

"Damn!" Mitch pounded the rail with his fist. "He owes me two hundred dollars!"

"Join the club," recommended the timekeeper. "You want your money back, you'll have to petition his estate."

"What about his wife?" Mitch had to raise his voice as the horse thundered past, clumps of dirt flying from its hooves. "Wasn't she a big film star back in the day? Seems to me she ought to be loaded."

"Oh, she ought to be," agreed the first man, turning back to the track to follow the horse's progress. "But whether the old man left her anything is another matter. Rumor has it he'd already been selling off her mementos to cover his debts. Unless you can prove a legitimate claim, you're not likely to see a dime."

"Just my luck," muttered Mitch, trying not to sound pleased that he'd just confirmed Frankie's theory.

"If you want to recoup some of your losses, here's a tip: Jazz Baby in the Saturday two-thirty," recommended the timekeeper, gesturing toward the horse rounding the far end of the oval.

"I'll bear it in mind," Mitch promised, then turned and walked away, trying to look like a man who had just lost two hundred dollars.

The sun was low in the sky by the time Mitch parked his car next to the curb in front of the Hollywood Studio Club and marched up the sidewalk with a spring in his step. Between his "date" the previous night and today's trip to Santa Anita, he had picked up a tidbit or two that Frankie might find interesting. Now, as he pressed the bell beside the front door, he looked forward to claiming his reward.

It was, to put it mildly, not what he expected. The door flew open to reveal the red-haired Roxie glaring at him with blood in her eye. "Oh, so it's you," she said in a voice that would freeze water.

"Hello to you, too," he said, puzzled by her hostile reception. He gave her what he hoped was a disarming smile. "Is Frankie in?"

For an answer, Roxie balled her fist and let fly, landing a solid punch to the left side of his nose.

"Hey!" Mitch staggered backwards, rubbing his abused face. "D'you mind telling me what *that* was all about?"

"As if you didn't know! Frankie is *in*, all right: *in* trouble, *in* the family way, and *in* over her head, all because of you!"

She advanced on him again, waving her fists menacingly.

"Whoa!" Mitch protested, grasping her flailing arms and holding them at a safe distance. "Hold your horses! Where'd you get an idea like that?"

"She told me herself she had an appointment today with Dr. Henry Winston."

"Is she sick or something?" asked Mitch, all at sea.

Roxie rolled her eyes. "Dr. Henry Winston, in case you didn't know, is one of the best-known abortionists in Hollywood."

Mitch had taken many hard hits on the gridiron over the years, but never before had mere words made him feel like he'd been kicked in the solar plexus, gasping for breath and unable to think straight. He almost wished Roxie had hit him again instead; it would have been less painful.

"And you think that *I*—that she—that we—"

"Who else would it be? Unless you're implying that she's the sort of girl who gets around, in which case I'll have to punch you again." She took a step closer, prepared to suit the word to the deed.

"I'm not the guy, Roxie, I swear. In fact, I can't imagine who—" But even as he said the words, he knew they weren't true. He could imagine who, all right. The one man who had the power to give Frankie what she wanted most of all. The same man who had then gotten himself killed, leaving her not only bereft of her dream, but forced to face the consequences alone. In that moment, Mitch fervently wished Arthur Cohen were still alive, just so he could have the pleasure of killing him himself, with his bare hands.

"Mitch, are you okay?" Roxie asked, all traces of anger vanished. "You look sort of strange."

"I feel sort of strange." He gave a shaky little laugh with no trace of humor in it. "After all, it isn't every day a guy finds out—"

"I'm sorry, Mitch, I really am. Honestly, I thought you knew." Roxie shook herself, and her voice became businesslike. "You'd better go home and get some ice on that bruise, or you're going to have a black eye by morning."

Mitch nodded absently. A black eye. If only that were the worst of his problems. He staggered back to his car and spent most of the evening driving aimlessly around Hollywood, not knowing or caring where he was going.

Frankie—*his* Frankie, the Snowy Soap Flake girl—was pregnant by a man old enough to be her father. Was that the real reason behind her determined search for justice? Poor Frankie! Even if she could bring Arthur Cohen back from the dead, he would never marry her. Mitch recalled that day in the library, when he'd had to explain to her what an abortifacient was. Had she known of her pregnancy then? Had he unwittingly offered a solution to her dilemma? While he'd been driving to Santa Anita, had she been lying on Dr. Winston's operating table while the blood of her unborn child—

No, he wouldn't think of it. Women sometimes died from such procedures, or were permanently scarred. There had to be a better way, and he would help her find it.

By that night, he knew what he had to do. He would marry Frankie himself and take her to Nevada with him, where no one would know her shameful secret. He would raise the child as his own and never utter a word of reproach. And if she should happen to give birth to a cigar-chomping, herbal tea-swilling brat in a pin-striped suit, well, he would love it if it killed him.

"What a day!" groaned Frankie, safe in the bedroom she shared with Kathleen. She stripped off her blue jacket and cast it onto the bed, then sat down on the edge of the mattress and kicked off her shoes.

Kathleen looked up from the little desk where she sat memorizing lines for her next audition. "Did everything go—" she paused discreetly— "all right?"

" 'All right' doesn't begin to cover it." Frankie leaped up from the bed and began pacing the small room. "Kathleen, I'm onto something here, something big. That Dr. Winston isn't a real doctor, at least, not the kind who helps sick people. He—well, he treats girls who are in trouble."

Kathleen went limp with relief. "You mean you didn't know? You're not—?"

"What sort of girl do you think I am?" demanded Frankie, torn between amusement and outrage at this insult to her reputation. "I only went there because I found Dr. Winston's telephone number on Arthur Cohen's desk. Kathleen, don't you see? Mr. Cohen could have gotten some actress in trouble—maybe even more than one—and sent them to this Dr. Winston."

Kathleen shrugged. "Like I told you, Frankie, some girls will do anything for a chance at stardom."

"But what if it didn't work out that way?" A shadow crossed her face as she remembered the young women in Dr. Winston's waiting room, their expressions showing varying degrees of anxiety and desperation. "What if afterwards she felt ashamed of what she'd done? Or what if Mr. Cohen went back on his word? Couldn't some poor girl see that as justification for murder?"

Kathleen laid her script on the desk and smoothed out the pages. "I don't know, Frankie, it seems to me an awfully big leap. Besides, even if it were true, how would you ever prove it? There's no way to prove paternity, you know."

Frankie sighed. "In this case, there's no way to prove maternity, either. Most of the girls seem to use false names. Unless—" She paused in her pacing as a new idea struck her.

"Unless what?"

"Unless I could somehow get a look at Dr. Winston's files. Surely those girls' real names must appear somewhere."

Kathleen raised a skeptical eyebrow. "Surely you don't expect the doctor's secretary to let you look through the file cabinet!"

"Actually," Frankie confessed, "I was thinking of breaking in."

Kathleen shook her head, making her blonde curls swing. "After what happened last time, Mitch said he was through with that sort of thing, remember?"

Frankie had the grace to look ashamed. "I wasn't thinking of Mitch."

"Who, then?"

"You."

"*Me*? You must be joking!" Seeing from Frankie's mulish expression that her roommate was quite serious, Kathleen added, "If you're determined to go through with this—and I'm not at all certain you should—you ought to tell that policeman friend of yours and let him handle it."

Frankie blushed crimson. "Kathleen! This isn't the sort of

thing you can discuss with a fellow!"

Kathleen did her best, but Frankie refused to be dissuaded. At last, the English girl reluctantly agreed to accompany her friend, expressing the not very hopeful opinion that she might somehow keep Frankie from bringing further trouble upon herself.

And so, long after curfew, both girls donned their darkest skirts and blouses and padded noiselessly down the stairs on stocking feet. They had a bad moment at the bottom of the stairs when they heard Pauline come in, late as usual, but they managed to steal into the shadows of the common room and remain out of sight until she had gone upstairs.

"Why did I let you talk me into this?" Kathleen hissed.

"*Shhh!*" was Frankie's only reply.

Once outside, they slipped on their shoes and hurried to the end of the block, where they had arranged for a taxi to meet them. Traffic was light so late at night, and it seemed a very short time later that they were set down at the corner a short distance from Dr. Winston's office. If the taxi driver was curious about their furtive behavior, he gave no sign, but Frankie tipped him generously anyway, just in case. They waited until the taxi had disappeared up the street, then Frankie unearthed a metal flashlight from the depths of her handbag and they walked up the sidewalk to the door of Dr. Winston's office.

Frankie had never been so thankful for its discreet distance from the street, or for the bushes that partially blocked its door from the view of passersby.

"Here, take this." She handed the light to Kathleen. "Shine it on the lock so I can see what I'm doing."

Picking a lock wasn't nearly as easy as Mitch had made it look. Frankie mangled two bobby pins before she finally heard a faint click and the doorknob turned in her hand.

"At last!"

The two girls scurried inside and Frankie locked the door behind them. Suddenly a blinding light filled the room. Frankie whirled around to see Kathleen with her hand on the light switch.

"Turn that thing off!" She gestured angrily. "Do you want to get us both arrested?"

The room went dark again, but not before Frankie caught a glimpse of Kathleen's stricken face.

"I'm sorry for snapping at you." Frankie's voice echoed in the empty room. "I guess I'm a little jumpy."

"Perhaps we should just go home," the British girl suggested.

"We can't give up now, not after coming this far." Frankie switched on her flashlight and played its beam against the adjacent wall until it illuminated the counter where she'd signed in that morning. "Come on, the office is this way. That's where the records will be."

Unfortunately for her quest, the door into the office was locked as tightly as the outer door, and this one proved even more resistant to Frankie's bobby pin. In the end, Frankie took off her shoes and clambered over the counter, then unlocked the door from the inside to admit Kathleen. The two girls found themselves standing before a receptionist's desk flanked by metal filing cabinets.

Frankie pointed to the one on the right. "I'll take this one, and you can have that one."

She pulled open the top drawer, cringing at the rasp of metal on metal, and began thumbing through the stacks of manila file folders. Half an hour later, she was almost ready to concede defeat. She'd had vague hopes of discovering a familiar name—Alice Howard, perhaps, who played Gwyneth in *The Virgin Queen*. Arthur Cohen had made some pretty nasty insinuations about her just before he died. But most of the girls who visited Dr. Winston chose to conceal their identities beneath false names. Besides the plethora of Smiths and Joneses, there were a couple of Jane Does and one Jane Q. Public. The only names that sounded remotely real were ones that had apparently been abandoned by their owners to conceal an unfashionable ethnicity or a blue-collar background, like Esther

Mertz or Ruby Mudd. Mudd? The ridiculous name was strangely familiar, but Frankie couldn't think where she might have heard it. She turned to her left, where Kathleen bent over a similar drawer of file folders, but even as she opened her mouth to ask her roommate for help, her memory provided the missing piece of the puzzle. She hadn't heard the name before; she had seen it scrawled in ink on the upper left-hand corner of an air mail envelope.

She stared at Kathleen for a long moment, debating her next move. At last she took a deep breath, and when she spoke her voice shook slightly. "Ruby?"

Kathleen glanced up, the instinctive reaction of one hearing the name she'd answered to for the better part of twenty years. Upon seeing the stricken look on Frankie's face, she realized her mistake. Her lips twisted in a humorless smile. "So you've figured it out at last, haven't you?"

Frankie remembered her arrival at the Studio Club, when she'd first met her roommate. On that occasion, Kathleen had been in bed with an unspecified illness. Had she really been sick, or was she recovering from Dr. Winston's procedure? Tears stung Frankie's eyes at the thought of her friend undergoing such an ordeal alone, separated by a continent and an ocean from family and friends who might have helped her.

"Oh, how awful for you," she breathed. "You must not

have known what else to do."

"I knew what to do, all right," Kathleen, or rather Ruby, said with a bitter laugh. "Girls used to come to my Granny all the time when they got in trouble. Married women too, them that didn't care to have a baby every year."

Every trace of her clipped British speech had vanished, and now she spoke with an accent not unlike Frankie's own. Frankie, her mind reeling, latched onto this relatively insignificant discovery. "You're not really English?"

"Not unless you count New London, West Virginia, population two hundred and twelve."

Feeling suddenly weak at the knees, Frankie groped for the edge of the cabinet for support. "But how—why—?"

"Because I knew there had to be more to life! Surely you ought to understand that, you felt the same way. I got married when I was fifteen—heaven knows there's nothing else to do in New London!—and my husband took me to Wheeling for a weekend honeymoon. One day we went to the movies, and *Grand Hotel* was playing." Kathleen's face grew radiant with the memory. "Oh Frankie, I fell in love that day, and I don't mean with my husband! For weeks afterwards, I would stand in front of the mirror and pretend to be Greta Garbo, acting out her part and reciting her lines."

"What did your husband think?"

Kathleen shrugged, dismissing her husband as of no importance. "Oh, he didn't know anything about it. I always waited until he was out working the farm. But I knew what I had to do. I saved up my butter-and-egg money for months until I had enough for the train fare, and then I just—left."

"You *ran away*?" Frankie's family hadn't been exactly over the moon about her desire to go to Hollywood, but Mama had taken her to Atlanta to shop for a suitable wardrobe, and Mama, Daddy, and both her sisters and their families had seen her off at the railway station. Now, hearing her roommate's story, Frankie hardly knew whether to be impressed with her bravery or appalled by her callousness.

Kathleen's chin jerked upward, a small yet defensive gesture. "I guess you could call it running away. It didn't feel like it to me, though. It felt like this was what I'd been waiting for my whole life."

"But—but how did you manage? What did you do when you got here?"

A faint, sad smile crossed Kathleen's face. "Funny thing is, I didn't even think of that until I was halfway across the country. Lucky for me, I met a man at the station. His name was Herbert Finch. He gave me my first big break."

Frankie felt a wave of resentment toward Mitch Gannon. If he hadn't stopped her from going with Mr. Finch, she might have had her first big break by this time, too. Trust him to spoil everything!

"What was the name of the picture?" she asked eagerly. "Just think, I might have seen you and never even known!"

Kathleen shook her head. "It wasn't—that kind—of film. I had five seconds on screen, dancing topless on a table."

Frankie's envious admiration turned abruptly to horror. "Kathleen, you didn't! Surely they used some sort of special effects—they wouldn't ask you to—"

"No, it was me up there, all right, in all my glory."

Frankie opened her mouth, but no words would come.

Kathleen, seeing her shocked expression, added quickly, "It was only the one time, until something better came along. There are so many girls looking for work in this town, if I hadn't done it, somebody else would have."

"But—but—"

"Besides," Kathleen added, squaring her shoulders proudly, "it paid off. Artie saw me in that film, and liked what he saw enough to offer me a contract with Monumental."

Frankie was scandalized all over again. "Mr. Cohen went to a—a—a *girly picture?*"

"It stands to reason he would want to scout out new talent," Kathleen insisted. "Oh Frankie, he was wonderful! He took care of everything. He gave me a new name, and a new life story, and he paid for speech lessons and took care of my rent at the Studio Club. He even promised me a leading role in one of his films. And all he asked in return was that I—"

"That you what?" demanded Frankie, very much afraid she already knew.

"It wasn't like I was a virgin!" Kathleen's voice rose on a note of hysteria. "I was a married woman, wed at fifteen because that was what my husband and my parents wanted. Well, what about what *I* wanted? Don't *my* wishes count for anything?"

Frankie patted the other girl's arm soothingly. "Of course they do." She smiled brightly, hoping to give Kathleen's thoughts a happier direction. "And he promised you a leading role? How wonderful! What's the name of the picture?"

Kathleen's snort of laughter held no hint of humor. "What else? *The Virgin Queen.*"

"I don't understand."

"Don't you get it? I was supposed to play Gwyneth, Queen Elizabeth's lady-in-waiting."

"But—but Alice Harper is playing Gwyneth," protested Frankie, growing ever more bewildered.

Kathleen's bravado evaporated. She heaved a heavy sigh and gestured toward the medical file in Frankie's hand. "I realized I was pregnant three weeks before casting began. I knew Artie would never marry me; there was never any question of that, even if he hadn't already been married to someone else. But I thought he might send me away to have the baby and arrange for it to be adopted."

"And he wouldn't?"

"He told me to get rid of it—no ifs, ands, or buts. He gave me Dr. Winston's name and address and said the studio would take care of the bill. Other than that, I was on my own." Her hands moved restlessly over the desk, found a silver fountain pen, and toyed nervously with it. "So I did it. I'd come too far, given up too much. This was my big chance! I couldn't let anything stand in my way."

Frankie saw the girl's increasing agitation, and as the pieces clicked into place she had the strange sensation that the ground had suddenly shifted beneath her feet. "When I met you, you were recovering from an illness," she recalled, afraid to hear what happened next.

"When you met me, I was recovering from an abortion," Kathleen said baldly. "When I returned to the studio to tell Artie the thing was done, I found out that not only had someone else gotten the part, they'd already started filming some of her scenes. He'd never meant to give me that part at all. He just wanted to get inside my knickers."

"Oh Kathleen, I'm so sorry," Frankie breathed.

Kathleen's lip curled maliciously. "Not half as sorry as Artie is."

The shifting ground suddenly opened, and Frankie stared horror-struck into the abyss. "Kathleen, you didn't—you couldn't have—"

"And why the hell shouldn't I, after what he'd done to me?" Kathleen's face contorted with rage. There was no longer any trace of the beautiful starlet, only a bitter young woman bent on vengeance. "I knew just how to do it, too. My granny knew a thing or two about herbs, and sometimes the local girls would come to her when they were in trouble. Some folks used it in small doses for an upset stomach—Artie even kept a canister of the stuff in his office. So I just smiled and said, 'Yes, Mr. Cohen, I understand, Mr. Cohen, that's show biz, shall I get you a cup of tea?' And I brewed that tea strong enough to abort a baby elephant. Only there was no baby there to abort, so he had to flush out his guts instead."

Her voice held a note of triumph, and she clearly expected a response. Frankie found her voice at last. "Mr. Cohen used you shamefully, but he didn't deserve to die."

"Neither do you, Frankie, but I have no choice."

Kathleen snatched the silver instrument from the desk, and Frankie realized that what she'd thought was a fountain pen was actually a scalpel. She backed slowly toward the door.

"You don't want to do this, Kathleen."

"I'm sorry, but I have to. After all I've done to be a star, after coming so close, I can't go to jail. If you won't fight me, I'll make it as quick and painless as possible. I owe you that much."

"I—I won't tell anyone." Frankie took another cautious step backwards. "Honest, I won't."

Kathleen gave a short laugh. "Do you really think we could just go back to the Studio Club as if nothing has happened? You wouldn't have to say a word. Roxie's a smart girl, and Pauline is no dope. They'd take one look at that baby face of yours and know the truth. Face it, Frankie, you're not that good an actress."

At any other time Frankie would have been offended by the slight to her acting skills, but at the moment it was the least of her troubles. "Let's not go back to the Studio Club, then," she coaxed. "Let's go to the train station and buy you a ticket back home. I'm sure your family is worried about you. If it's money you need, I'll help—"

"I *can't* go back, don't you see that?" Kathleen's voice rose hysterically. "I threw away the love of a good man and whored myself out for the chance to be a star. I killed my own baby! I've come too far, Frankie. There's no turning back for me. Not now. Not ever."

Still wielding the scalpel, she slowly advanced two steps as Frankie retreated, the synchronized movements resembling a macabre dance.

"You can't get away with it, Kathleen. The other girls will ask questions when you return to the Studio Club without me."

Kathleen's gaze faltered for just a moment, then she nodded as a solution presented itself. "I'll tell them you were in trouble. They know you had an appointment with Dr. Winston this morning. I'll tell them you wanted to get rid of the baby, but couldn't go through with it and killed yourself instead."

Frankie took another step backward. And bumped into the wall. In her terrified retreat, she had lost her bearings and misjudged the position of the door. In the time it would take for her to glance behind her to locate it, Kathleen would be upon her. Even as the thought crossed Frankie's mind, she saw Kathleen's eyes flash, and knew she was thinking the same thing.

Having gained the advantage, Kathleen pounced on it, seeming to leap across the empty space between them. Frankie flung up her arm to ward off the surgical knife and felt a burning pain as it sliced through the flesh of her forearm. Kathleen drew the scalpel back for another blow. Before she could strike, the crash of shattering glass filled the room. A moment later, a familiar figure loomed up behind Kathleen.

"Mitch!" Frankie cried. "Be careful, she's got a—"

As Kathleen slashed wildly at the air, Mitch caught her arms and wrenched them behind her back. The blade slipped from her fingers and fell to the floor, spinning across the linoleum until it came to rest against a foot clad in black patent leather. Officer Russ Kincaid stood framed in the doorway, his pistol trained on the girl struggling in Mitch's unloving embrace. The policeman's eyes never wavered from his target as he bent to pick up the scalpel at his feet, then stepped aside to allow two more uniformed cops to enter the room in his wake.

"Be careful, boys, she's like a cornered animal—she's got nothing left to lose. Hang on to her, Gannon, while we get the cuffs on her."

Mitch was glad to oblige. "Good timing," he told Kincaid as the sobbing Kathleen was led from the room in handcuffs. "What tipped you off?"

"The taxi driver thought something wasn't quite right about his fares wanting to be set down outside Dr. Winston's office in the middle of the night. His description of one of the girls matched Miss Foster, and knowing her history of breaking and entering for a good cause, I decided I'd better check it out. What about you? What made you follow her?"

Remembering his erroneous assumptions about Frankie's condition, he darted a sheepish glance in her direction. She sat huddled where she had fallen, cradling her bleeding arm to her chest. Her face was white as a ghost, and she stared blankly into space, apparently unaware of anything going on around her.

"I just played a hunch," Mitch answered with a shrug. "Now, since you've got your hands full with Kathleen, I'd better get Frankie to a doctor. That arm needs attention."

Kincaid opened his mouth as if to protest being saddled with a criminal while his rival walked away with the girl, but duty won out. He gave Mitch a curt nod, then followed Kathleen and her captors out of the room.

Alone with Frankie, Mitch took her gently by the elbow and raised her to her feet. "Hey, kid, come on. We'd better get that arm looked at."

Frankie, released from her trance, burst into tears. "Oh, Mitch! Oh, Mitch!"

Mitch had faced down two-hundred-pounders on the gridiron without a second thought, but the sight of a crying female filled him with terror. He wrapped his arms around her and patted her awkwardly on the back. "Hush, kiddo, it's all right now."

Trembling violently, Frankie sobbed something unintelligible into the front of his shirt. The only word Mitch could understand was "Kathleen."

"I wouldn't worry about her if I were you," he said

soothingly. "She'll probably get off with an insanity plea. Who knows? The insanity might even be real."

"Real?" Frankie lifted her head from his shoulder and raised her tear-stained face to his. "Nothing in this God-forsaken town is real! Everyone's as phony as those fake buildings on the back lot. It's nothing but a bunch of unscrupulous, scheming, immoral, selfish people who don't care what they have to do or who they have to step on! All the beauty and magic you see up there on the screen, it's only make-believe. None of it is real!"

She collapsed onto his shoulder and dissolved into tears once more. None of the comforting things her murmured into her hair had any effect beyond making her cry even harder. Finally, in desperation, Mitch tried a different approach.

"Real? Of course it's not real!" He grasped Frankie by the shoulders and gave her a little shake. "You want real? Real is settling down with that nice boy whose mother plays bridge with yours every Wednesday afternoon. Real is growing old bragging about your glory days fifty years ago, when you sang the Snowy Soap Flake jingle on the radio."

Frankie opened her mouth to protest, but Mitch held up a hand to forestall her.

"Okay, maybe you're right. Maybe there are a bunch of shady folks in Hollywood. But the amazing thing is that those immoral, selfish people—and the good ones too, let's not forget them—somehow manage to create something that makes the whole country laugh, or cry, or sing, or dance. That's where the magic is. That's what made you travel all the way across the country to be a part of it."

Taken aback by this burst of eloquence, Frankie pondered Mitch's words for a long moment. It was true that Hollywood housed more than its share of horrible people, like Arthur Cohen and Herbert Finch and, yes, even Kathleen. But there were good people too, people like Roxie and Russ. There was Miss Williams, directress of the Studio Club, who ran a place for girls to live so they wouldn't be dependent on men like Herbert Finch. And there was Mitch, who was always there for her, even when she didn't want him to be. She swiped at her tears with the back of her hand, then looked up at him with a wobbly smile that erased all the terror and grief of the last hour.

"Thank you, Mitch. You always know just what to say."

EPILOGUE

Stand Up and Cheer (1934)
Directed by Hamilton McFadden
Starring Shirley Temple

A hush fell over the crowd filling Grauman's Chinese Theater as the elaborate crimson and gold curtain swept open to reveal the big blank screen behind it. Frankie, carefully avoiding the sight of the empty seat on her left where Kathleen should have been, turned slightly to her right and squeezed Mitch's arm.

"This is it," she whispered.

Then the lights dimmed, the big screen flickered to life, and the recent tragedy receded, at least for a couple of hours. "Monumental Pictures presents . . ." the words on the big screen read, "THE VIRGIN QUEEN, in glorious Technicolor!" The crowd "oohed" and "aahed" at the vivid hues projected onto the screen, colors so bright they cast red and blue reflections onto the faces of the audience. The cast and crew had worked at a frantic pace over the last few weeks, re-shooting every scene with the new cameras that were able to film in color. Maurice Cohen had even paid a small fortune to cast the award-winning British actress Barbara Payne as Queen Elizabeth. To judge from the audience's reaction, all their efforts had not been wasted.

Frankie, however, hardly noticed the rich brocades of Barbara Payne's costumes or the swelling violins of the theme music, although both were rumored to be Oscar contenders. Her sole interest lay in two scenes: the crowd scene where she made up part of the mob cheering the queen's arrival, and the tavern scene where she'd distributed tankards of fake ale as a serving wench.

"I think that's my arm," Frankie whispered urgently to Mitch. "See it? Right there!" She pointed toward the screen, where the arms of over one hundred extras (most of which looked just alike to Mitch) waved in greeting to the queen.

"Er, I'm not sure," hedged Mitch, reluctant to disappoint her.

Before she could pinpoint the location further, the picture on the screen switched to a close-up of Barbara Payne in full Queen Elizabeth regalia.

Frankie's face fell. "Oh well, I'm sure there'll be a better shot of me in the tavern scene."

But the tavern scene was a long time in coming. At last, almost ninety minutes into the film, Miss Payne commanded her dewy-eyed lady-in-waiting in throaty accents, "Take this message to Leicester at once! You will find him at the Rose and Crown."

Frankie sat upright with a jerk and leaned forward in her seat. "This is it!"

Up on the screen Alice Harper, in Gwyneth's page disguise, opened the door and slipped inside what appeared to be a tavern, although Frankie knew it was actually a façade built on the back lot and its seemingly solid half-timbered walls didn't stretch more than six feet on either side of the door. A moment later the door opened again, and William Stanford burst through with much waving of sword.

"My horse!" he commanded a cowering stable lad. Seconds later, he thundered away from the tavern on his trusty steed with Gwyneth riding pillion behind him.

Frankie stared at the screen in dismay. "They cut it!" The swell of the music drowned out her stunned protest. "They cut my big scene!"

The last half-hour of the pictures passed in a blur of flickering images. Frankie was blind to the stirring sword fight and didn't even notice when Gwyneth fell into Leicester's passionate embrace while Queen Elizabeth, having lost the man she loved, smiled tragically yet regally down upon them from her throne. At last the picture faded to black, leaving only large white letters reading "In Memory of Arthur G. Cohen, 1881-1936." Then the house lights came up and the audience, blinking against the sudden brightness, started heading for the exits.

When they reached the red-and-gold splendor of the lobby, Mitch turned to Frankie with a grin. "I liked the sword fights, but I suspect my history prof from A & M wouldn't recognize half of it."

"I can't believe they cut my big scene," Frankie moaned. "I knew I wouldn't be the center of attention, but I never expected the entire scene to end up on the cutting room floor. What am I going to tell my family? Everybody back home thinks I'm halfway to being a star."

Mitch gave her a sympathetic look. "Chin up, Frankie. There'll be other pictures."

"Maybe." Frankie grew pensive, thinking of Kathleen and all she'd given up for a chance at stardom. "Or maybe I'd be better off taking the next train back to Georgia."

"What do you think of Nevada?"

Frankie blinked at Mitch. "What?"

Mitch shoved his hands into his trouser pockets and jingled his loose change. "I said, 'what do you think of Nevada?' I've been offered a job there, we could—"

"There you are!" Maurice Cohen, dressed for the occasion in a tuxedo, separated himself from the cluster of people surrounding Barbara Payne and hurried over to join Frankie and Mitch. He took Frankie's hands.

"Miss Foster, I feel I owe you an apology. After all you did for the studio, and for my family, it seems very poor thanks that we should cut your scene out of the film."

Frankie, touched in spite of her disappointment, tried to summon up a smile. "Oh well, I guess that's show-biz."

"Indeed, it is. In fact, the film had to be heavily edited for length. We had to cut out several scenes in order to keep the film under two hours. Audiences won't sit still for longer than that."

"I'm sure no one could get tired of watching Miss Payne," Frankie said wistfully, glancing over to where William Stanford draped a fur stole over the star's shoulders.

"You may be right," the younger Mr. Cohen agreed with a smile, seeing the direction of her gaze. "Still, it's always best to leave the audience wanting more. I do wish to make it up to you, though. In a week or two we'll begin filming a college musical called *Fraternity Row*. I'd like to use you as one of the sorority girls, if you're interested. It's not a big part—maybe half a dozen scenes, with a couple of brief lines of dialogue and perhaps a little dancing, if you're able to pick up the choreography."

Frankie's eyes grew round, and her jaw all but hit the floor. "Me? You want me to speak lines? And dance?"

Mr. Cohen held up a hand to silence her. "I know what you're thinking, and I don't blame you. But I can assure you this is not a matter of charity. You looked good on the rushes—the camera obviously likes you. You earned another chance, and I intend to see that you get it."

"Why—why, thank you, Mr. Cohen," Frankie stammered. "Thank you very much!"

"Ed Reynolds will be directing. If you'll stop by his office Monday morning, his secretary can fill you in on the shooting schedule. Now, I know you two must have plans for the evening, so if you'll excuse me, I'll say goodnight."

Frankie stared after him as he returned to the crowd surrounding Miss Payne, then wheeled back to face Mitch. Her eyes were aglow, and her hands clasped together beneath her chin.

"Oh Mitch, can you believe it? My first speaking role! I can't wait to tell Roxie, and I'll have to write a long letter to Daddy, and—but what were you saying before we were interrupted? Something about Nevada?"

Mitch shook his head. "Never mind," he said, draping his arm across Frankie's shoulders as they headed for the exit. "It wasn't important."

ABOUT THE AUTHOR

Sheri Cobb South is the award-winning author of fifteen novels, including Regency romances *The Weaver Takes a Wife*, *Miss Darby's Duenna*, and *Of Paupers and Peers*. She has also written a number of teen romances for Bantam's long-running Sweet Dreams series. She made her mystery debut in 2006 with the publication of *In Milady's Chamber*, which introduced Bow Street Runner John Pickett. Sheri has always loved classic Hollywood movies, and hopes to convey a similar comic tone in her writing. A native and lifelong resident of Alabama, she recently moved to Loveland, Colorado, where she is currently writing a third John Pickett mystery. Sheri loves to hear from readers. Visit her website at www.shericobbsouth.com, "like" her on Facebook, or email her at Cobbsouth@aol.com.

DISCARDED BY HEMPSTEAD PUBLIC LIBRARY

DISCARDED BY HEMPSTEAD PUBLIC LIBRARY

13287712R00137

Made in the USA
Charleston, SC
29 June 2012